THE NIGHT ATTACK

Behind her a twig crunched. Rosemary spun and saw a vague shape detach itself from a cluster of cottonwoods and glide soundlessly toward her. How the warrior had gotten behind her was a mystery, but he had, and odds were that other Sioux were converging and would overwhelm her at any moment.

She would go down fighting, Rosemary resolved. She had never thought of herself as particularly brave, but she refused to go meekly into eternity. She refused to turn the other cheek, not after what the Sioux had done.

Rosemary sighted down the rifle, but the bead was indistinguishable from the darkness. The best she could do was point the muzzle at the center of the advancing figure and hope she scored. Ever so slowly, she thumbed back the hammer. Another ten feet and she would fire. The Sioux would be so close, she couldn't miss.

Without warning arms encircled Rosemary from the rear and held her tightly....

The Wilderness series:

#1: KING OF THE MOUNTAIN
#2: LURE OF THE WILD
#3: SAVAGE RENDEZVOUS
#4: BLOOD FURY
#5: TOMAHAWK REVENGE
#6: BLACK POWDER JUSTICE
#7: VENGEANCE TRAIL
#8: DEATH HUNT
#9: MOUNTAIN DEVIL
#10: BLACKFOOT MASSACRE
#11: NORTHWEST PASSAGE
#12: APACHE BLOOD
#13: MOUNTAIN MANHUNT
#14: TENDERFOOT
#15: WINTERKILL
#16: BLOOD TRUCE
#17: TRAPPER'S BLOOD
#18: MOUNTAIN CAT
#19: IRON WARRIOR
#20: WOLF PACK
#21: BLACK POWDER
#22: TRAIL'S END
#23: THE LOST VALLEY
#24: MOUNTAIN MADNESS
#25: FRONTIER MAYHEM
#26: BLOOD FEUD
#27: GOLD RAGE
#28: THE QUEST
#29: MOUNTAIN NIGHTMARE
#30: SAVAGES
#31: BLOOD KIN
#32: THE WESTWARD TIDE
#33: FANG AND CLAW
#34: TRACKDOWN
#35: FRONTIER FURY
#36: THE TEMPEST
#37: PERILS OF THE WIND

#38
WILDERNESS

MOUNTAIN MAN

David Thompson

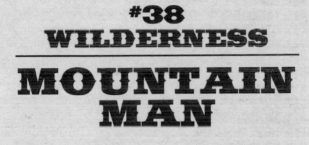

LEISURE BOOKS NEW YORK CITY

Dedicated to Judy, Joshua and Shane.

A LEISURE BOOK®

December 2002

Published by

Dorchester Publishing Co., Inc.
276 Fifth Avenue
New York, NY 10001

ISBN: 0-8439-5071-4

The name "Leisure Books" and the stylized "L" with design are trademarks of Dorchester Publishing Co., Inc.

Printed in the United States of America.

Visit us on the web at www.dorchesterpub.com.

MOUNTAIN MAN

Chapter One

Faith was the key. A person must always have faith.

Rosemary Spencer had it to spare. She had faith in her husband, Bert. Faith in his decision to uproot their family and trek overland more than a thousand miles to the Promised Land, or Oregon Country, as it was known. She had faith in their children, fifteen-year-old Sam and nine-year-old Eddy, faith they were mature enough to endure without complaint the hardships they would encounter. She had faith in their team of oxen, in the plodding, steadfast, tireless brutes on whom their lives depended. She had faith in the new Conestoga the oxen were pulling, in its sturdy construction and reliability. But most of all, Rosemary had faith in their Maker. God Almighty would see them through to Oregon, would see to it they reached their homestead in the Willamette Valley with their scalps and hides intact.

Their wagon train was two and a half weeks out of Fort Leavenworth, paralleling the sluggish Platte River.

David Thompson

In all her born days, Rosemary had never imagined so much grass existed. A great, rollicking sea of greenish brown, unending wave after unending wave, the stems ceaselessly rippled by the breeze. Gazing out across its limitless expanse, she could well believe it went on forever, although she knew better, knew that eventually the formidable Rocky Mountains would rear before them and they would come to South Pass, their gateway over the Divide, and to their new future.

Humming happily, Rosemary resumed knitting. In the creaking seat beside her sat Sam, her oldest. His sandy hair spilled from under his floppy hat, and Rosemary made a mental note to give him a trimming in the next day or two. He caught her glance and smiled, his sunburned face speckled as always with dozens of freckles.

"Ain't this something, Ma?"

"*Isn't* it something," Rosemary corrected him. "And yes, dear, it is." Her boys saw the journey as a grand adventure. Ever since Bert made the announcement at supper several months ago, they had been bubbling over with excitement.

At first, Rosemary hadn't shared their enthusiasm. That night, after she had tucked the boys into bed, she'd sat in her rocking chair on the front porch and listened awhile to Bert puff on his pipe in the darkness. At last she had made bold to comment, "I wish you had let me in on your plans, Bertram. I have a lot to do to get ready."

Bert stopped puffing and shifted on the porch step. "I just made up my mind this morning, Rose. Folks have nothing but praise for Oregon. They say it never wants for rain, and the soil is so rich crops practically grow themselves."

Rosemary had gazed across their yard at their barn and the cornfields beyond. Their farm was modest, but she loved it, loved their quaint house, loved hearing the rooster crow in the morning and their cows low in the evening. Forty acres wasn't much, but it had been her father's, and his father's before him, and it was enough for them to get by. "This land has been in my family for generations."

"I'll get you more land out to Oregon," Bert boasted. "One hundred and sixty acres for every settler. Four times as much as we have now." He'd taken his pipe from his mouth. "I've already got a buyer and sealed the deal."

A twinge of apprehension gripped Rosemary. "Who, might I ask?"

"Pringle."

Harvey Pringle's huge farm abutted theirs, and he had been after Bert for years to sell. But of all the people in the world, Rosemary would rather it were someone else. She had never liked Pringle, never liked how he looked at her with those hungry eyes of his, and how he contrived to brush his grossly overweight body against hers whenever they met in town or when he came to visit.

"He's offering us top dollar," Bert had gone on, then he told her the price. "Twice what the land is worth. Of course, I have to throw in the cows and chickens, and he gets to harvest the corn. That's fair, don't you think?"

Rosemary's hands had tightened on the arms of her chair. Her husband, bless his soul, had the business sense of a tree stump. A fairer price would be three times as much, but she had smiled and said softly, "Yes, dear."

Now Rosemary was glad she did. Things had gone without a hitch. The sale had gone through on time. Bert had bought a brand-new wagon in town, and Pringle let him have a team of oxen for half price, "out of the goodness of my heart," as Pringle put it.

The jumping-off point to the uncharted frontier was bustling Independence, Missouri, at the other end of the state from Holstein, where she had been born and spent her entire life. But it might as well have been a whole new world. Rosemary had marveled at the colorful ebb and flow of humanity: energetic townspeople in dapper suits and elegant dresses; steely-eyed gamblers in black frock coats and wide-brimmed hats; bronzed frontiersmen in fringed buckskins. Most remarkable of all were the Indians, members of peaceful tribes who came to trade. Civilized Indians, some called them. Tame Indians, others said. But to Rosemary they didn't seem particularly civilized or tame, and she couldn't stop thinking of the brutal atrocities Missourians had suffered at red hands before the last of the uprisings were put down. She saw tall, stately Mandans, with finely chiseled features. She saw painted Pawnees, their hair cropped into crests down the center of their heads. And there were Osages, too, miserable wretches whose tribe was pitiably poor, and who were the laughingstock of the other tribes and whites, alike.

They all made Rosemary's skin crawl. She couldn't help it. She tried not to let their presence bother her, but she kept remembering her grandfather.

Bert had asked around and learned a wagon train was leaving for Oregon within the week. It was late in the season, and he had been worried there might not be another until next spring. But the old man at the stable had introduced them to Harry Trapp, and now here they were, the last of nine wagons rolling in single file across the prairie.

The sun was warm on Rosemary's face, the scent of grass reminiscent of alfalfa. She hummed louder and tried not to think of the warning the owner of the general store had given them. Bert had gone there to stock up on provisions, and when the proprietor learned where they were bound, he had motioned them aside.

"Listen, it's none of my business, but you seem like nice folks, and I'd hate for anything to happen to you."

"How do you mean, Mr. Carpenter?" Bert had asked.

"You're better off waiting until next year. It's September already. Snow comes mighty early to the high country, and once you're past South Pass, you're taking your life into your hands." Carpenter had turned his back to the other customers and lowered his voice. "For another thing, your train is too small. There won't be enough men to ward off an Indian attack, if it comes." He'd lowered his voice still further. "And there's something else. Something between you and me. Something I'll deny if you tell anyone." Carpenter paused. "Your wagonmaster doesn't have the best of reputations. Last year about this same time he took twelve wagons out and only half made it through to Oregon."

Bert had thanked the man, and later, at Rosemary's insistence, they had gone to Harry Trapp and questioned him. The pilot was a lanky rail of a man whose beard needed trimming and whose clothes were in bad need of a washing. He had listened impatiently to Bert, then swore.

"Who's been filling your ears with this hogwash? Some townsman, I bet, who's never set foot on the prairie in his life." Trapp had drawn himself up to his full height. "I've led fourteen trains to Oregon. Fourteen! And the one time some pilgrims were lost along the way, I never hear the end of it."

"What happened to them?" Rosemary had inquired.

"Stupidity, ma'am," Trapp responded. "They were killed by their own stupidity. They thought they knew better than me. Halfway to Oregon we passed through a nice little valley with plenty of grass and water. They decided they'd rather settle there than go the rest of the way."

"Why would they do that?" Bert asked.

"They were tired, Mr. Spencer. Tired of being on the go twelve hours a day. Tired of the heat and the bugs. Tired of the toil." Trapp had looked at each of them in turn. "I won't lie to you folks. There are no guarantees any of us will reach Oregon alive. There will be long stretches where water is mighty scarce, and game scarcer. There are Injuns to deal with. Grizzlies, buffalo, wolves. A hundred and one things that can kill you dead if you don't keep your mind on what you're doing. For every ten pilgrims who make it to Oregon, there's one or two who don't."

"Those people who wanted to settle halfway there?" Rosemary prompted when he fell silent.

"Oh. I almost forgot." Trapp scowled at the memory. "I talked myself blue in the face, but they wouldn't listen. They insisted on staying. I had no choice but to go on with the rest, so I left them." His scowl deepened. "On the way back, I stopped to see how they were doing. They were dead. Wiped out. Every last man, woman, and child."

"My word," Bert said. "Who was to blame?"

"Hostiles. I couldn't tell which tribe. But it wasn't a pretty sight, I assure you. And some gents hereabouts have held it against me ever since."

"It wasn't your fault, though," Bert declared.

Harry Trapp smiled and placed a hand on her husband's shoulder. "You're a man after my own heart, Mr. Spencer. Try telling these townsmen that, though. Some claim I'm a bad wagonmaster, but there are wagonmasters who have had more people die on them than I have." He winked conspiratorially. "The truth of the matter, if you ask me, is that it hurts the merchants where it matters most. They're getting rich selling provisions and they're afraid they'll lose business. Afraid if word gets out, fewer folks will head to Oregon."

His explanation had seemed reasonable to Rosemary. Bert and her discussed it at length and decided to see their adventure through to the end.

"Ma!" a youthful voice hollered from the rear of the wagon, bringing Rosemary's reverie to an end. Twisting, she beheld her youngest leaning out the back of the Conestoga and pointing to the south. "What is it, Edward?"

"Are those buffalo, you reckon?"

Rosemary squinted against the harsh glare of the late-afternoon sun. Sure enough, on the far horizon were several vague dots, but whether they were buffalo or something else was impossible to say. "I don't rightly know," she admitted.

"Shucks," Ed muttered. "We ain't ever going to see any "

"*Aren't* going to see any, son," Rosemary amended. "And don't give up hope. Mr. Trapp mentioned last night we should see some any time now. Soon we'll be in the heart of buffalo country."

"And Indian country," Sam casually mentioned. "I sure would like to get a redskin in my rifle's sights."

Rosemary didn't like being reminded. "Don't talk like that. Some Indians are friendly. With a little luck we won't run into any who aren't."

"We owe them for what they did to Grandpa," Sam said.

"We can't blame the Indians who live out here for what happened back there," Rosemary surprised herself by saying. Normally, she was the last person to defend the red race. But fair was fair.

"That's not what you said last year," Sam mentioned. "You told Mrs. Jacobson that you agreed with the man in the newspaper who wrote the only good Indian is a dead one."

"It was the heat of the moment." Rosemary had been arguing with a neighbor lady over whether Indians should be rounded up and pushed onto reservations, or exterminated, as many were calling for.

"Call it what you want, Ma," Sam said. "I still want to get a red devil in my sights."

Rosemary didn't appreciate it when her son talked that way. She wasn't one of those who hated Indians on general principle. She had a reason. They had slain and mutilated her grandfather, the sweetest, kindest soul who ever lived, a man so gentle he refused to carry a gun, even after hostilities broke out.

From near the left-rear ox came her husband's stern reprimand. "Don't ever let me hear you sass your mother like that again, Samuel. You're never too old for a tanning. Show her the respect she deserves."

Rosemary had almost forgotten Bert was there. As was customary, he was walking beside the team to better control them, and when necessary, he would goad the dumb brutes with a flick of his twenty-foot whip. The six oxen were plodding mechanically along, their huge heads bowed in their yokes. They were arranged in pairs, the largest two nearest the wagon to bear more of the load.

And what a load it was! Every article of value Rosemary and her family owned, every household item and personal effect, was piled in the Conestoga's ten-foot-by-three-foot body. Almost five tons of it, Bert had estimated. Heavier possessions were on the bottom: their plow, their dresser, their stove, her spinning wheel. Next came their clothes and tools and utensils. On top were things they used every day—a cooking pot, sacks of flour and salt, axes, blankets—and in one corner the long rifles they might need to defend themselves.

Their wagon, Rosemary had noticed, was a bit larger than the rest in the train. The others were prairie schooners, shorter, lighter versions of the Conestoga. She was glad her husband hadn't bought one. As it was, she had been forced to sell or give away far too much.

Her mother's piano, her grandmother's loom, and more had to be sacrificed in order to meet the weight limit.

The thought of spending months cooped up in a Conestoga hadn't appealed to Rosemary one bit, but she had to admit, as time went by she realized it wasn't all *that* bad. There was enough room left for them to sleep inside in inclement weather. The heavy canvas top, saturated with linseed oil to make it waterproof, would keep them dry should it ever rain. It also spared them from the worst of the blistering sun and sheltered them

8

from the high winds that invariably ripped across the plains each evening.

The wagon's hardwood bed was another marvel of construction. Able to withstand great abuse, it was supported by massive axles and a sturdy undercarriage. Theirs had a steel kingpin, the pivot that enabled the wagon to turn, and was far superior to the iron kingpins of the prairie schooners.

All in all, Rosemary was proud of the Conestoga, and proud of her husband for choosing it over the smaller models. He had spared no expense, as he often reminded her, in order to make the trip less taxing on her and the children.

Bert was such a good husband. His decision to sell the farm aside, Rosemary had always trusted his judgment.

Then Harry Trapp came riding back from his usual position on point. Wheeling his sorrel, he nodded at Rosemary and said to Bert, "You're falling behind again, Mr. Spencer. You're doing a lot of that of late."

"I'm pushing the oxen," Bert responded, hefting his whip, "but they're tired."

"No, they're just plain slow," Harry Trapp said. "Everyone else has mules, and mules make better time. You would have been smart to buy mules too."

Bert's jaw muscles twitched, as they always did when he was angry. "Now you tell me. Why didn't you mention this back in Independence?"

Trapp shrugged. "It's not my place to tell people how to live their lives. I figured you'd do a better job of keeping up, even if your oxen are older than they should be—"

"Old?" Bert interrupted. "You must be mistaken. My neighbor, Harvey Pringle, assured me these animals are in their prime."

"I don't suppose it was this Pringle fella who sold them to you, was it?"

"What does that have to do with anything?"

"Only that he must be chuckling to himself right about now," Trapp said, and sighed. "I can't slow the whole train on your account. Push your critters harder, or by nightfall you'll wish you had."

"Surely you're not suggesting you would abandon us?" Bert said, laughing lightheartedly at the preposterous notion. "I have a wife and children."

"All the more reason to keep up," Trapp insisted, and scanned the rippling waves of grass. "Especially during this next stretch. A month or so ago some Sioux were seen in the vicinity."

"Sioux?" Bert repeated, sounding as if he had accidentally swallowed an apple.

"They stray down this way now and then to hunt buffalo and lift a few scalps." Trapp caught himself and glanced at Rosemary. "Not that I'm expecting trouble, ma'am. The Sioux don't have many guns, and they're not fools. They won't brace us so long as we stick together and stay alert."

Rosemary watched him ride back up the line, her heart aflutter with anxiety. Bert cracked his whip a few times and the oxen plodded a trifle faster. "Pringle swindled us, selling us these animals," she commented. Just as he had swindled them out of a fair price for their farm. Her husband didn't answer. Flushing red, he snapped the whip at the lead ox.

"Get along there! Get along!"

Rosemary bent to her knitting. She needed to keep busy, to keep occupied, to take her mind off a knot of dread forming deep inside her. But her heart wasn't in it, and after a few deft flicks of the needles, she balled the swatch of would-be shawl, swiveled, and placed it in the wagon.

Both her sons wore worried expressions. Sam was gazing anxiously across the prairie.

Ed was gnawing on his lower lip, a habit of his when he was upset.

Smiling to reassure them, Rosemary said, "Have faith, boys. Things will work out. Mr. Trapp and the others won't really desert us. No one can be that unspeakably wicked."

"It's the Indians I'm thinking of, Ma," Eddy said. "I've heard stories."

"We all have," Rosemary said. "But as Mr. Trapp mentioned, they're not likely to attack us, not with all the guns we have. So quit fretting." Adopting a nonchalant air, she reached for her shoulder bag and removed her hairbrush and small mirror.

Rosemary had her own habits. As a little girl she had picked up one that stuck with her to this day. Whenever she was troubled, whenever she had a lot to ponder, she would brush her hair, stroking it over and over while she contemplated. It helped her think, helped clarify problems and find solutions.

Now, holding the mirror up, Rosemary regarded her face. Bert was always complimenting her on how pretty she was, but she knew better. She was plain as plain could be. Her nose was much too thin, her cheeks weren't full enough. Her lips had a perpetual pout to them that Bert seemed to like but which lent her a child-like aspect she wasn't fond of. Her blue eyes were her best feature. Deep, aqua blue, like the blue of a beautiful lake on a summer's day. Over the years she had received a few compliments about her hair, too, but it was too fine to suit her. Here, under the blazing prairie sun, her blond tresses shone with uncommon luster, falling in gradual curves well past her slim shoulders.

Rosemary swiped at them with the brush and soon settled into a rhythm. Her mind drifted on currents of random thought. She pictured Pringle, pictured thrusting a pitchfork into his keg of a belly, and inwardly grinned. He deserved it. He surely did. Greed and lust were all that motivated him. She never had understood people like that, people who used others, people who didn't care whom they hurt. Her conscience would never let her cheat someone as Pringle had cheated them.

The Conestoga gave an abrupt lurch, and Rosemary had to grip the seat to steady herself. A small hole was to blame, an old prairie dog burrow eroded by the elements. She glanced back at the large wheels on her side of the wagon, making sure they were intact. They were, of course. It would take a lot worse than that to damage them. The massive hubs were nigh indestructible. From them radiated heavy spokes that fit into sockets in the outer rims. The rims themselves were made up of curved sections, the felloes, that fit seamlessly together, and were in turn ringed by an iron strip, known as the tire, that protected them from wear and tear.

Rosemary gazed along the trail in the direction they were heading. The famous Oregon Trail was a broad, rutted track, the soil riven by the countless wheels of the many hundreds of wagons belonging to all the wagon trains that had gone before theirs. Trapp had told them this was the easy part of the journey, that later, beyond South Pass, the country changed, becoming mountainous and rugged and arid for long spells, and would stay that way until they reached their destination.

The Promised Land. The land of milk and honey. Rosemary wondered if Oregon, and the Willamette Valley in particular, were really the paradise everyone made them out to be. Supposedly, the climate was mild year-round. Even in winter the grass was green, and heavy snowfalls were a rarity. Crops flourished, the earth was so rich. And best of all, the Indians were friendly.

Rosemary daydreamed about their grand new farm, envisioning their new house, painted bright green as she liked, with neatly trimmed flower beds and tall trees for shade. She would have a vegetable garden, with string beans, lima beans, and asparagus. Potatoes. Pumpkins. Melons. The bounty of the land, courtesy of the Lord.

"We're falling behind, Ma."

Sam's comment caused Rosemary to look up. The sun was perched on the rim of the world, and the shadows of the wagons and oxen ahead had lengthened considerably. It wouldn't be long before Harry Trapp would call a halt for the night. She noticed, with gnawing alarm, that the other wagons were several hundred yards ahead. It wasn't a lot, but sufficient for her to feel keenly vulnerable. Should hostiles attack, the Indians would swarm over their Conestoga before help could arrive.

Rosemary was relieved when, in due course, the pilot drew rein and pumped his arm overhead, the signal for the wagons to pull into a circle. Room was left for theirs, and by the time they arrived the other men had removed their mules from harness and the women were preparing supper.

Trapp came over as Bert was unyoking the oxen. "I'm beginning to worry a mite, Mr. Spencer."

"I'm doing the best I can," Bert said, and once again groused. "I wish you had told me about my animals before we started out. I could have taken steps."

"Like what?" Trapp said a trifle testily. "Sell your oxen and buy mules? There wasn't a spare team to be had, or I'd have suggested it."

Bert's lips compressed into a thin line. "Still, it was remiss of you not to warn us. I paid you two hundred dollars to be our guide. Our welfare, our very lives, are in your hands."

"Are you implying I'm only interested in the money?" Trapp snorted. "Hell, if that was all I cared about, there are easier ways to earn it. Piloting pilgrims is the most thankless job around. Up before sunrise, in the saddle from dawn until dusk, never enough sleep, never enough food, hostiles and silvertips everywhere."

"I wasn't implying anything of the sort," Bert said defensively.

Trapp glanced at Rosemary and the boys, hesitated a moment, then said, "Listen, Mr. Spencer. I explained the risks to you. I laid out all the rules a wagon train has to abide by. One of those is that everyone must keep together. It's one of the most important of all. I was as honest as I could be, and I'm being honest with you now. We're too far out for you to turn around and go back alone. Push those oxen of yours harder tomorrow. Please. For all our sakes." He walked off.

Ed had crawled to the front of the Conestoga. Tugging on Rosemary's sleeve, he asked, "Are we in trouble, Ma?"

"Not at all," Rosemary assured him. "The oxen will hold up, you'll see. Six months from now we'll be seated at the dinner table in our new home and look back at this day and laugh."

"I hope so, Ma," said Sam, hopping down to give Bert a hand.

To the west the sun was being slowly devoured. Soon ebony night would fall. Rosemary felt a shudder run through her, and she couldn't say whether it was the cool breeze that had sprung up or something else entirely.

Chapter Two

As was customary, at five A.M. the man on sentry duty fired his rifle into the air and everyone was required to rise and shine.

Rosemary disentangled herself from Bert and shuffled sleepily to the front of the Conestoga. Pulling a robe on over her heavy woolen nightgown, she stiffly climbed out and kindled the fire. Other women were doing the same. Like them, she climbed back inside to rouse the children and dress.

Bert was up, tugging on his trousers. He had to join the men and help gather the wagon teams and horses, a task that usually took half an hour. Pulling his short-brimmed hat low over his eyes, he pecked her on the cheek and hustled out.

Rosemary touched her cheek in mild surprise. Her husband rarely displayed affection. She could count the number of times he had kissed her in public on two hands, and the number of times he had done it in front of the children on one. Not that he didn't care. Far from it. He adored her with the breadth and depth of his soul. But there was a time and a place for everything, and affection was properly the province of the bedroom. Or so Bert had instructed her early on in their marriage.

Rosemary never gave it much thought. Most husbands, she had discovered, weren't all that different. Where romance was involved they were horrendously shy, almost comically awkward. Men had a natural aversion to sharing their feelings. Why that should be was one of life's many mysteries. She figured it was how the Good Lord had made them, and let it go at that.

The next two hours passed eventfully. Breakfast had to be cooked and consumed. Those who had slept in tents instead of in their wagons had to strike the tents and pack everything away. Teams had to be hitched. Harry Trapp insisted on being under way by seven each morning, and he brooked no delays. Families piled into their prairie schooners, whips were cracked, yells rent the brisk morning air, and the wagon train was once again in motion.

Rosemary liked to stretch her legs first thing, so she walked beside Bert for an hour or so. Most mornings they hardly exchanged ten words, but today he coughed to clear his throat and gave her a peculiar look.

"Samson was limping a bit earlier."

"Oh?" Rosemary glanced at the ox in question. The entire team had names, courtesy of her boys, and Samson was paired with Solomon closest to the wagon. "He's not limping now."

"I know. Just thought I would mention it," Bert said.

"What else is on your mind?" Rosemary probed. She knew her man as thoroughly as she knew herself.

"While I was gathering up the team, Mr. Weaver came over. He wanted me to know a secret vote was taken last night."

"Secret vote?" Rosemary didn't like the sound of that. "Whatever about?"

"Us. Harry Trapp called the other men together late last night after we had turned in. He explained how we are slowing everyone up. How if it keeps up, he'll be lucky to get the train through to Oregon before the snows hit."

Appalled, Rosemary gazed toward the front of the train where the pilot sat astride his sorrel. Anger bubbled within her, anger so potent it was all she could do not to march up to him and demand he apologize for his atrocious behavior.

"He had the men take a vote on whether to push on without us if we fall too far back," Bert detailed.

"Surely they wouldn't vote to leave us," Rosemary said. No humane, civilized person could be so heartless, so unspeakably cruel.

"Weaver wouldn't tell me the outcome," Bert said, "but he begged me not to fall behind again." Bert frowned. "That tells me a lot right there."

Rosemary took his hand in hers and squeezed. Her husband had a tendency to get down in the doldrums when life threw obstacles in their path. She, on the other hand, saw them as challenges to be overcome. "Everything will work out," she predicted. "Wait and see."

"Have I ever mentioned how greatly I admire you?"

Surprise was piling on surprise. Rosemary's husband was as stingy with praise as he was with kisses. "Not recently," she bantered, troubled more by his sudden change in character than she would have been were he acting true to his usual self.

"You're always so confident, so positive things will turn out as you want them to turn out. I try to be more like you, but I can't. It's just not in me."

"All it takes is faith." If Rosemary had a motto, that would be it.

"Easier said than done," Bert commented, staring skyward. "Some of us have more questions than answers, more doubts than convictions."

"Are you implying you don't believe?" Rosemary asked, aghast. Why, the entire seventeen years of their marriage she had always taken it for granted he did.

"Quite honestly, I'm not sure. Ever since Doug and his family died, I haven't known what to believe."

Doug was Bert's older brother. He had lived in Wisconsin, and on a dark and frigid night in mid-December two years ago his house had caught fire. No one made it out alive. Not Doug, not his wife Marcy, not any of their three children, all daughters, delightful cherubs as sweet and innocent as could be.

"Bad things happen," Rosemary said. "That's just how life is."

"How convenient for the Almighty," Bert said bitterly. "As excuses go, it's rather feeble." He went to say more but changed his mind and walked a few steps ahead, cracking his whip over the heads of Cain and Abel, the lead oxen.

Rosemary's steps faltered. "Lord, grant me strength," she breathed, and slowed so the wagon came up alongside her. Without breaking stride she slid up onto the lazy board, her legs dangling. Reaching higher, she gripped one of the ties to the canvas canopy. Inside the Conestoga Sam and Ed were doing their morning studies, Ed reading aloud as was his wont, carefully pronouncing each word. She mentally closed her ears and leaned her forehead against the side.

For all Bert's praise, Rosemary wasn't the pillar of confidence he believed. She had doubts, just like everyone else. When they bothered her the most, when she was tempted to think that maybe, just maybe, the naysayers were right and she was wrong, she would withdraw deep within herself until the temptation passed and she was in her right mind again.

For half an hour Rosemary clung to her perch, ab-

sorbed in prayer. Only when she heard her sons arguing
did she stir and slide off the lazy board. Moving to the
rear of the wagon, she gripped the top of the loading
gate and swung herself up and over. The boys stopped
arguing immediately. She started to move forward, but
her dress had become snagged between the canvas and
the gate. Prying it loose, she was about to turn when she
happened to glance eastward—and froze.

A lone rider was following them. A mile back, maybe
more, the horseman was silhouetted against the azure
sky.

Rosemary shaded her eyes with one hand and tried to
tell whether he was white or red. The distance was too
great to be certain, but one thing was for sure: He was
wearing buckskins. Indians favored them, but so did
frontiersmen.

"Who's that, Ma?" Eddy was at her side, squinting
into the sun. "One of the company?"

"I don't think so," Rosemary answered. Only six of the
ten men owned horses, and they generally stayed close
to the train unless Trapp sent them on ahead to forage
for game or wood.

"It's a redskin, I reckon!" Eddy excitedly declared.
"Want me to holler for pa to shoot the varmint?"

"He's too far off," Rosemary said. "We'll keep an eye
on him, though, and if he comes any closer we'll let
everyone know."

Sam joined them. Leaning on the gate, he peered intently at the haze-shrouded figure. "Whoever he is, he's
a big one, Ma."

"You can tell from here?" Rosemary never ceased to
be amazed at her oldest's exceptional eyesight. He had
the eyes of an eagle, and could see things others couldn't.

"Yes, ma'am," Sam confirmed. "Him and his horse,
both. He doesn't seem to be in any hurry."

"Take turns watching him," Rosemary directed as she
worked her way front, moving along the narrow space

they had left for just that purpose, and remembering to step over the plow handle. Once on the seat, she picked up her knitting and for the rest of the morning busied herself with the shawl she was making.

Rosemary glanced back now and again and the big rider on the big horse was always there, always holding to the same distance.

It was customary for wagon trains to stop for an hour in the middle of the day, as much to rest the teams as anything else. Their nooning this day was on a grassy flat beside the gurgling Platte. "A mile wide and an inch deep" was how the river was routinely described, a joke testifying to the fact that as rivers went, it was downright puny.

Rosemary glanced back once more as the wagons were rumbling to a stop. The rider had gone, as mysteriously as he appeared. She searched the prairie but saw no sign of him, and she felt a strange sense of disappointment.

Sam came up as she was climbing down. "That jasper rode off into the buffalo grass as soon as Mr. Trapp yelled for us to stop. I doubt he's a redskin, Ma. No Indian would ride out in the open like he's been doing."

Rosemary had reached the same conclusion. "Maybe he's a frontiersman," she speculated. "On his way the Lord knows where."

Eddy came scrambling over their possessions to the seat. "I've always wanted to meet one, Ma. Folks says they're snake-mean and will stomp you if you so much as look at them crosswise."

Rosemary glanced up. Of them all, Edward had the most vivid imagination. It explained why he loved to read so much. But she had to keep an eye on him. Once, she caught him with his nose buried in one of those awful penny dreadfuls. Filled with lurid tales, the stories were rife with violence and scantily clad maidens in dire distress. Ridiculous tales, fit only for simpletons and hopeless romantics. "Folks say a lot of things that aren't necessarily true, son."

"Could be he's one of those mountain men," Eddy said. "Maybe on his way back to the Rockies."

"I saw a mountain man in Independence," Sam piped in. "He had real dark skin and eyes like none I've ever seen. I asked a clerk about him, and the clerk told me his kind pass through Independence from time to time." Sam paused. "The clerk also said most people are afraid of them. Mountain men are as tough as grizzlies and as friendly as rattlers. The clerk's very words."

"Gosh," Eddy said, eyes widening. "Let's hope he comes closer."

"You two have chores to do," Rosemary reminded them. "Whoever that man is, he's keeping to himself and minding his own business. I suggest we do the same."

Their noonday meal was a hasty affair. It had to be, since they would be under way by one o'clock. Rosemary prepared soup and plenty of piping-hot coffee for Bert. He could drink it by the gallon, laced with sugar so thick it was sweeter than hard candy. They had filled their bellies and Bert was leaning back to light his pipe when Harry Trapp walked up.

"I'm glad to see you've kept up with us this morning."

"Told you we would," Bert said.

Trapp turned to Rosemary. "Pardon me, Mrs. Spencer, but I overheard your boys telling some of the other boys that you saw a rider back yonder?"

Bert lowered his pipe. "What's this?"

"That's true, we did," Rosemary said. "He was there most of the morning."

"And you didn't think to let me know?" Trapp asked in a less-than-pleasant tone. Before she could answer, he went on. "I thought I'd made it plain this is dangerous country. Not just because of Injuns, neither. We never know who we'll run into out here. Cutthroats and half-breeds are as common as ticks on a coon hound, and

David Thompson

they'll rob you blind or slit your throat with no excuse at all."

"Honestly, Mr. Trapp," Rosemary said. "Aren't you exaggerating a wee bit? It can't be as bad as all that."

"If you only knew," Trapp said softly, more to himself than to her, then said sternly, "If you see the rider again, you're to get word to me. Have one of your younguns run up the line. Or send your husband. It's important I know. Is that understood?"

Rosemary resented being treated like a child. "I understand perfectly. Never fear. I don't make the same mistake twice."

"Very well." Trapp tilted his head back and scrutinized the vault of blue overhead. "It's going to be a scorcher today. I'd hoped, starting this late in the season, that the weather would be cooler. But sometimes it stays hot clear into November." Touching his hat brim, he ambled toward another family.

Bert was staring at her. "You should have said something. To me, at least."

"I don't see why everyone is making such a big fuss," Rosemary responded. "Nothing happened. The man went his way and we'll go ours."

"That's not the point and you know it."

Yes, Rosemary did know it. She freely admitted to herself she had made a mistake, but she would be darned if she would admit it to Harry Trapp. His constant prodding and lectures were becoming a trial.

Sam and Eddy returned from visiting some of the other children and Rosemary put them to work cleaning up and loading the pot and utensils. She was snippy with them, and they looked at her in hurt confusion. Later, after the wagons were under way, she felt bad about it and asked them to join her in song. They sang several church hymns, including "Rock of Ages," and a ditty the boys liked about a farmer and his cow. She was grinning and relaxed for the first time that day when Eddy abruptly pointed eastward, out the rear of their Conestoga. "He's back again, Ma."

Rosemary twisted around. There he was, the big rider on the big horse, the same distance away as before. His buckskins were plain in the sunlight, but little else was discernible. "Tell your father," she instructed her oldest.

Sam vaulted lightly to the ground. Bert was up near the lead oxen. When Sam relayed the news, Bert sent him racing up the line to inform Harry Trapp.

The pilot rode back at a gallop. Wheeling his sorrel, he paced their wagon and stared over his left shoulder at the man in the distance. Rosemary wondered why he didn't go question the rider in person.

Seconds later Bert drifted to the rear and asked, "What do you make of him, Mr. Trapp? Is he a threat to our loved ones?"

"I'll know more in a minute." Opening a saddlebag, Trapp removed a brass spyglass, telescoped the tube to its full length, and raised the eyepiece to his right eye. He studied the rider awhile, then announced, "By the looks of him, he's a mountaineer."

"A what?" Rosemary asked. The term was new to her.

"Sorry. That's what the mountain men call themselves. Mountaineers." Trapp nodded at the rider. "My guess is he's on his way home after paying civilization a visit."

Burning with curiosity, Rosemary said, "May I have a look? I've never seen a mountain man before."

Trapp leaned toward the Conestoga. "Be my guest. But they're not much different than anyone else. Saltier and smellier, is all."

Rosemary fiddled with the eyepiece, adjusting it just right. An image took shape, the image of a broad-shouldered man with raven-black hair and a trimmed black beard. His footwear consisted of knee-length moccasins. Slanted across his wide chest were a powder horn, an ammo pouch, and a fair-sized leather bag, its purpose unknown to her. A rifle rested across his saddle

23

and a brace of flintlock pistols were tucked under his brown leather belt. On his right hip was a large knife. On his left was what appeared to be a tomahawk. "He's a living armory," she commented.

"Mountain men have to be," Trapp said. "Without their weapons they wouldn't last a month in the high country."

Rosemary noticed something odd about his clothes. "Are those beads on his shirt and pants?"

"Sure are. Injuns are fond of decorating their buckskins with 'em. My guess is he has an Injun gal tucked away somewhere. A lot of his kind do."

"They marry red women?" Bert interjected, making it sound as if it were a cardinal sin.

"Mountain men need companionship, same as everybody else," Trapp said. "Some turn completely Injun and give up the white man's world permanent-like."

Sam had returned and was listening attentively. "Ain't that wrong? I mean, they're red and we're white."

"To some people, boy, color doesn't matter as much as it ought to." Trapp accepted the telescope from Rosemary. "The old-time trappers were the worst. They didn't care who they took up with. Bridger, Meek, Walker, they all took Injun women. Meek lived with his wife's people for years, until it got so you couldn't tell him from a redskin." Trapp was replacing the spyglass into his saddlebag. "Not all that long ago there was a black feller, a member of the Lewis and Clark expedition, who took up with the Crows. They must think highly of him, because the last I heard, they'd made him a chief."

"I'd never live with Indians," Sam said.

"Me either," the pilot declared. "But I don't hold anything against those who do. I've always been a strong believer that folks should be able to do as they please so long as it doesn't harm anyone else."

"Don't forget the Ten Commandments," Bert threw

in. "There are some things we shouldn't do, no matter what."

"Like 'Thou shalt not kill'?" Trapp said with a hint of sarcasm. "Tell that to a hostile about to lift your hair. The Ten Commandments don't apply west of the Mississippi. Not if you want to live to reach the Promised Land alive."

Rosemary was angry the pilot would speak like that in front of her children. "I'll thank you to keep your personal opinions regarding Scripture to yourself. We've taught our children to live by the Golden Rule at all times."

"With all due respect, ma'am," the pilot said, "turning the other cheek on the frontier is the same as asking to push up clover. All it does is make you easier to kill."

Rosemary glanced at her husband for support, but Bert was staring at the ground, so she pressed the case herself. "Mr. Trapp, you've been at your job too long. You've forgotten what truly matters in life. Forgotten our purpose for being here."

"What would that be, ma'am?"

Clear and loud, Rosemary said, "To love our neighbors as we love ourselves."

Harry Trapp's eyebrows met over his nose. "I admire you, ma'am, and those like you. Honest to God I do. But it seems to me you're looking at the world with blinders on, sort of like those horses that pull carriages in big cities. Loving a neighbor is all well and good, but I don't see how that applies to Injuns. A lot of tribes are about as neighborly as rabid wolves. And they're heathens, to boot. Their gods ain't the same as ours. They don't believe the same things we do. So it's damned silly to sit there and talk about loving them."

"I'll thank you to watch how you talk to my wife, sir," Bert broke in. "Show more respect, if you please."

"No insult intended, Mr. Spencer," Trapp said. "I'm

only trying to make her see that her ways aren't the ways of the whole world."

"Be that as it may," Rosemary said, "I'll live as I deem best, and the rest of the world be hanged."

Trapp looked rather regretfully at each of them in turn. "I pray to God you people don't learn your lesson the hard way," he said, and raised his reins to ride off.

Bert wagged his whip to the east. "What about the mountain man?"

"What about him? He's minding his own business, we'll mind ours." The sorrel departed in a cloud of dust.

"I don't know as I like him, Ma," Eddy commented.

"Some people are harder to get along with than others," Rosemary said, and let it go at that. Deeply troubled, she resumed her knitting, but her heart wasn't in it. Her gaze strayed to the mountain man. She wondered what motivated a man like that. Why had he forsaken his own kind? Why did he live in the wilderness, hundreds of miles from the nearest town or settlement?

With a toss of her blond hair, Rosemary stopped troubling herself over a total stranger and glanced at her husband. Bert was walking beside the nearest pair. His hand on Samson, he had bent low and was examining the animal's foreleg. "Is something the matter?"

"He's limping again."

Rosemary watched closely. It was barely noticeable, but every third or fourth step the ox favored its left foreleg. "He's not doing all that bad."

"Yet," Bert said. "Tonight I'm wrapping the leg to keep it warm. You can help me out by making a compress of those herbs you use to heal sprains and such."

"Will they work on an ox?" Rosemary asked, and was startled out of her skin when her husband spun on her, his face contorted in suppressed fury.

"Why must you carp all the time? Can't you see I'm doing the best I can? Just make the compress and let me know when it's ready."

"Bertram!" Rosemary had never seen him so mad. "What has gotten into you? I didn't criticize—" But he wasn't listening. His spine as stiff as a ramrod, he marched to the head of the team and cracked the whip with renewed vigor. Bewildered by his uncharacteristic behavior, Rosemary slumped in the seat, her emotions awhirl. In all the years they had been together, he had never turned on her like that.

"Is Pa all right?" Sam inquired in a small voice.

"Why'd he talk to you like that, Ma?" This from Eddy.

Struggling to compose herself, Rosemary mustered a smile. "It's the strain, boys. It rubs a body's nerves raw. He'll be fine by the time we stop for the night. Wait and see."

The afternoon was as hot as the pilot had predicted. The temperature climbed upward of one hundred degrees, by Rosemary's reckoning. She was sweltering. From under the seat she procured a fan and sought to cool herself.

All afternoon the rider shadowed them, always at the same distance, always holding to the same gait. Brushy country flanked the river, and gullies and washes were a lot more common.

It was later than usual when Harry Trapp signaled for the train to circle up. The emigrants went through their usual evening ritual. By nightfall cookfires were blazing, guards had been posted, and younger children were scampering about at play. A man from Virginia—Morris, his name was—brought out a fiddle and entertained them.

Bert hardly spoke ten words to Rosemary. They sat on stools near their wagon, Bert smoking his ever-present pipe, she with her knitting.

Harry Trapp, Roemary noticed, was a bit edgy. He prowled the circle like a caged cougar, stopping often to peer into the darkness. What he was looking for, he never said.

David Thompson

Rosemary put down her knitting and rose to add a few limbs to the fire. Earlier she had piled the firewood her boys gathered near the rear wheel, and as she bent over the pile she saw a pair of feet in the shadows. Moccasin-clad feet. Her gaze roved upward and her breath caught in her throat. It was him!

The mountain man!

Chapter Three

Rosemary Spencer started and stumbled several steps backward. Unreasoning fear spiked through her, and she raised a hand to her throat. Inadvertently, she bumped into Bert, nearly knocking him off his stool. The contact steadied her, both outwardly and inwardly, and she stifled a budding outcry.

"What the devil?" Bert blurted, throwing out his legs to brace himself. "What's gotten into you, Rose?" Turning, he came up off the stool as if it were a red-hot coal. "It's him!" he exclaimed.

Their fellow travelers were so busy chatting or engrossed in listening to the fiddler that no one else noticed the mountain man until he strode into the firelight. Almost instantly, all talk ceased. The music died on a strangled note. Halting, the mountain man calmly surveyed the encampment.

Fascination replacing her fear, Rosemary drank in every detail of his appearance. Through the spyglass he had seemed big; up close he was a giant. His shoulders were broader than any man's there, his chest as big around as a barrel. Yet his waist was deceptively thin. He moved with an ease and economy of motion suggestive of a cat. The beads on his buckskins glistened in the play of firelight, as did the rifle cradled in his thick arms and the pistols under his belt. He had an air about him Rosemary couldn't quite define. An air of confidence, and something more. The image that leaped to her mind was of a wolf among sheep, but that wasn't quite right. It was more like a great bear among a bunch of cubs. The way he walked, the way he looked at them, it set her heart to fluttering, but whether from apprehension or another emotion, she couldn't rightly say.

Surprisingly, the mountain man was undeniably handsome. To Rosemary, at least. His face was extraordinarily pleasing. A high brow hinted at high intelligence, and below it were piercing green eyes that missed nothing. His gaze roamed full circle and settled on her, and for a few puzzling moments her insides turned to water and her knees went oddly weak.

Rosemary noticed new things about him, little things not obvious through the telescope. His buckskins were clean and well-kempt, his face devoid of grime. A thin necklace of blue beads graced his neck. Some of his hair had been twined into a slender braid at the back of his head, and from the braid hung an eagle feather.

The mountain man smiled, displaying white, even teeth, and in a voice that rumbled from his chest, said amiably, "Evening. My apologies for disturbing you folks. I hope you don't mind my paying you a visit."

Rosemary's admiration mounted. He wasn't at all the uncouth lout she had been led to believe.

Everyone glanced toward Harry Trapp. The pilot had been as shocked as everyone else, but he now came forward wearing a smile and offering his hand. "You're more than welcome to join us, friend. Trapp's my handle. I'm wagonmaster for this outfit."

"King," the mountain man said as he shook. "Nate King."

Rosemary saw Trapp give a start, then glance at the man's hand as if taken aback by the strength in the other's grip.

"Have a seat, why don't you?" the pilot said, and scanned the ring of faces, apparently trying to decide which family to join. To Rosemary's consternation, mixed with a dollop of delight, he pointed at their fire, which was nearest.

"Do you mind, Mr. and Mrs. Spencer?" Trapp said.

Bert rose. "Not at all," he said cordially. "Please, Mr. King. Be our guest. I'm sure my boys would love to meet you."

Sam and Eddy were cross-legged by the wagon, their lower jaws hanging down to their knees.

Nate King smiled and sank down with his back to the Conestoga, sitting in such a fashion that he was facing their fire but not gazing directly at it. Placing his big rifle across his thighs, he said, "I could smell your cook fires from half a mile off." He looked at Harry Trapp. "So could anyone else, but I reckon some things can't be helped."

Trapp nodded, and Rosemary had the impression a secret tidbit of information had passed between them.

King gazed with wry amusement at Sam and Eddy. "I have two sprouts of my own. Pleased to meet you gentlemen."

Eddy jumped to his feet so fast, his empty plate clattered to the ground. "How do you do, sir," he said, thrusting out his hand. "You're the first mountain man I've ever met. Are they all as big as you?"

"Not all of them, no," Nate King said, a twinkle in his eyes. "One coon I know is so small, he can fit through a keyhole."

Eddy laughed, and emboldened by his success, asked, "Why do you wear that feather in your hair? Have you taken up Indian ways?"

Rosemary was scandalized by her youngest's lack of manners. "Edward! Don't pester the poor man."

"It's all right, ma'am," King said quietly. "My own kids were fountains of questions at his age." The big man reached behind him and stroked the feather with what Rosemary could only describe as reverence. "A Cheyenne warrior gave me a feather just like this once, back when I was new to the frontier. It was a token of friendship, of respect. I've long since worn out the original, but I like to wear one to remind me that just because people have different skin color doesn't mean they can't be friends."

"Oh," Eddy said, as if the explanation were more than he bargained for. "So you must like Indians a lot."

Again Rosemary sought to correct him. "Edward, I won't tell you again."

Nate King wasn't offended at all. "I guess I must," he informed her youngest. "I'm married to an Indian lady, and her people have adopted me into their tribe."

Sam rose and moved closer. "No fooling, mister? Which tribe is it? Do you go on raids with them?"

Eddy had another question of his own. "Have you taken any scalps?"

Shoving erect, Rosemary put her hands on her hips. "That will be quite enough out of both of you! I simply will not have you badgering our guest."

"The answer to both questions is yes," the mountain man said.

For an uncomfortable minute no one said a word. Rosemary filled a tin cup with hot coffee and gave it to King, who cradled it in both big hands and blew on it before taking a sip. His green eyes scanned the camp again, his brow knitting, and it seemed to Rosemary he was trying to come to some sort of decision.

Harry Trapp's forehead was also creased. "I've heard your name before," he broke the silence. "Usually mentioned in the same breath as Bridger and McNair."

"Friends of mine," King said.

"Shakespeare McNair is still around? Why, he must be pushing ninety. They say he was one of the first. That he's lived up in the mountains longer than any other white." Trapp was making small talk, but it was as plain as the nose on his face that he had another subject he wanted to broach and was hesitant to do so.

"McNair was the first," Nate King confirmed. "He took me under his wing when I came west and taught me enough to keep me alive." King peered over his steaming cup at the pilot. "One mistake is all it takes."

"I do the best I can," Trapp said. "I try to take everything into account, but I'm only human."

The mountain man nodded at the Spencers' Conestoga. "This wagon, for instance. It's too big, and too slow. A turtle on wheels. Fit for travel back east, but not out here." His tone hardened a trifle. "You should have told them."

Trapp spread his hands, palms out. "There's only so much I can do. I mentioned about the wagon before we left. But I can't help it if people don't take my advice."

Rosemary realized the pilot must be referring to Bert. Trapp had never mentioned anything about the Conestoga being too large to her. She glanced at her husband, and he looked away.

Eddy, overcome by awe, had plunked down in front of the frontiersman. "This is our wagon, Mr. King."

"I know. I saw your brother and you watching me."

"You did?" Sam said skeptically. "How could you see us from that far out without the help of a . . ."

"Spyglass?" King finished for him, and chuckled. "Live out here long enough and your senses become sharper than you can imagine."

"You saw the telescope?"

"I saw the sun reflect off the casing every time you spied on me. It wasn't hard to figure out what it was." King sipped more coffee, then lowered the cup. "Indians might have mistaken it for a rifle and attacked you. Remember that. Out here even the smallest blunder can get you killed."

Eddy held his hand aloft as if he were back in the one-room school in Holstein. "Mr. Trapp says we're in Sioux country and we have to be mighty careful."

"Mr. Trapp is right." King glanced at the pilot, then at Rosemary, and finished his coffee in a quick gulp. "I'm obliged for the hospitality, but I should be getting along. My horse is off in the grass by his lonesome. It wouldn't do to leave him unattended."

"Please stay a while yet," Rosemary heard herself say. "Have you eaten? We have some stew left. I'm not the best cook in the world, but my menfolk never complain."

Nate King bent toward the pot and sniffed. "My nose tells me you're too modest, Mrs. Spencer." Straightening, he tilted his head and appeared to be listening. "I reckon half an hour more won't hurt. I've had to eat my own cooking for so long, I've forgotten what real food tastes like."

Scooting to find another plate, Rosemary heard Eddy say, "Tell us more about Indians. My ma and my brother think the only good redskin is a dead one."

Rosemary stopped cold in her tracks. Her youngest was smiling in benign innocence, but Sam looked as if he were trying to shrink down into the earth. Bert's corn-cob pipe was producing enough smoke to rival a forest fire, while Harry Trapp was out-and-out dumbfounded.

"Do they, now?" Nate King said. It was impossible to judge by his tone what he was thinking.

"I saw some friendly Indians in Independence," Eddy warbled on. "Pawnees, and some Mandans, I think. Oh. And some Osage. They were a scrawny lot." Eddy propped his elbows on his knees and his chin in his hands. "Did one of those tribes adopt you?"

"No, the Shoshones."

"I never heard of them. What are they like?"

Rosemary bustled to the wagon, her emotions in turmoil. What must King think of them now, after her youngest's slip of the tongue? His opinion must have dropped to rock bottom, and it was a wonder he didn't up and leave. Maybe the boys were keeping him there. She sensed he liked children. Having two of his own, perhaps he understood not to take their comments too seriously.

Retrieving a plate and spoon, Rosemary rounded the wagon in time to hear an intriguing remark.

"—ever harmed a white man. Same with the Flatheads. Most people only ever hear about the hostiles. About all the blood spilled. The lives lost. But what about the Flatheads, who saved a starving band of trappers back in the winter of '32? Or the Shoshones, who will bend over backwards to make whites welcome in their villages?" Nate King's next statement was directed at Sam. "Before you go around branding someone as deserving to die, walk a mile or two in their moccasins."

"I didn't mean all Indians," Sam said meekly, "It's just that our grandpa was killed by redskins and—"

King held up a hand. "I'm sorry for your loss, boy. Sincerely sorry. There's been too much blood spilled on both sides, and I'm afraid a lot more will be spilled before people come to their senses."

Rosemary moved to the cooking pot, which hung from a tripod over the low fire. Conscious of the mountain man's scrutiny, she ladled a heaping portion onto the plate and carried it over to him. She couldn't bring herself to look him in the eyes, not after Eddy's comment. But she should defend herself. She didn't want him believing she was a bigot. "I hope—" she said, and had to swallow. Her throat was unaccountably dry. "I hope you won't think poorly of us. I was mad when I made that foolish statement. I loved my father very much. I miss him to this day."

Nate King was a few moments replying. "We all say things we shouldn't when we're angry. You should have heard me the last time I stubbed my toe."

Relief washed through Rosemary, and she bestowed a warm smile. The mountain man wasn't at all what she had expected. He wasn't coarse or uncouth or mean. Quite the contrary. He was considerate and understanding, rare qualities in the best of men. And he had a marvelous sense of humor.

"Tell us more about the Shoshones," Eddy urged with typical childish enthusiasm. "What's it like being married to an Indian lady?"

Rosemary's elevated spirits crashed to earth. "Will you never learn, Edward?" she said in exasperation. "There are some things people don't talk about."

"Like what, Ma?"

Chuckling, King leaned back. "I don't mind. There are about five thousand Shoshones. Whites call them the Snakes. They claim a large territory drained by the Snake, Bear, and Green Rivers. Most live in villages, in hide lodges, and every ten days or so they move their villages to new sites. They dress in buckskins. The men are well-proportioned, the women are quite attractive."

"Do they take scalps?" Eddy inquired.

Rosemary sank onto her stool. Belatedly, she saw that everyone else had stopped what they were doing to listen. Embarrassment flared anew, and her cheeks grew warm.

"On occasion they do," Nate King admitted. "So do the Crows, the Piegans, the Bloods, the Utes, and a dozen other tribes I could name."

"A barbaric practice," someone commented.

King never looked around. "When I first came to the frontier, I thought so, too. But they don't do it out of bloodlust. To them a scalp is a symbol, a token of bravery in battle. The more scalps a man has, the higher he rises in the tribe. They call it counting coup."

"Are we to gather you condone their savagery?" an older woman sniffed accusingly.

"If by condone you mean approve, then no, I don't," King said. "But I'm not going to hold it against them, either. We can't judge the Shoshones or any other tribe by our standards. Their world is completely different."

Charley Kastner snorted. "Sounds to me like you're making excuses on their account because you're married to a squaw."

A complete hush fell. Rosemary tensed for an explosion of violence. "Squaw" was considered an insulting term, akin to calling a white woman a "tramp." Nate King sat rock-still for all of five seconds. Then he slowly rose and turned, his rifle level at his waist. With measured tread he strode over to Charley Kastner. The muzzle an inch from Charley's nose, he said politely, "I'd like an apology."

Kastner was an outspoken, brawny fellow in his early thirties who liked to throw his stocky weight around. He also liked to brag about how tough he was, and how many fistfights he had been in. He claimed there wasn't an Indian born he was afraid of, and that if hostiles ever attacked the wagon train, they'd regret tangling with Charley Kastner, by God. But now he was scared, and it showed. To his credit, though, he looked down the barrel of the mountain man's weapon, moistened his lips, and said, "It's a free country. A man can say what he damn well pleases."

"Out here," King said, a nod encompassing the untamed world that lay beyond their sheltering ring of wagons, "what a man says can get him killed."

Charley Kastner's throat bobbed. "You're bluffing. You wouldn't kill me in front of all these women and children." When King failed to respond, Charley smirked and declared, "I didn't think so. Why, if you weren't

37

holding that Hawken on me, I'd gladly thrash you within an inch of your life."

Keen disappointment knifed through Rosemary as Nate King stepped back and lowered his rifle. She thought he was backing down, but instead he handed the Hawken to Harry Trapp, then slid both pistols from under his belt and handed them over, too. Balling fists the size of a sledge, he planted himself a few yards in front of Kastner.

"Whenever you're ready."

Beads of perspiration formed at Charley Kastner's hairline. He started to rise but sat back down and jabbed a finger at Trapp. "What kind of pilot are you that you let a stranger waltz in here and cause trouble? Isn't it your job to protect us?"

Trapp nodded. "I agreed to protect you from Injuns and wild critters. You flap your gums at your own risk."

Kastner glanced from right to left for support that never came. His wife said, "Don't do it, Charley!" but he ignored her as he generally ignored her anyway.

"I'm waiting for my thrashing," Nate King said.

Every nerve in Rosemary's body tingled with expectation. She didn't honestly expect Kastner to stand up. He was mostly bluff, a bag of hot air that could use puncturing. But he possessed a kernel of grit somewhere, because the next moment he shot toward the mountain man as if fired from a cannon.

King met the rush head-on. He blocked a looping right, ducked a high left, and retaliated with a quick jab to the jaw that rocked Kastner onto his heels. Charley shook his head to clear it, then barreled back in again, swinging furiously. There was no method to his assault. He relied on his bulk and his strength, and perhaps that was enough against most men. If his claims were true, it had enabled him to come out on top in over three dozen fights. But this time he was up against someone considerably bigger and immensely stronger.

Nate King slipped punch after punch, evaded blow after blow. He did so easily. When he moved, he was a blur. And when he swung, he connected.

Charley's sweaty moon face acquired a lump on the temple, a bruise under an eye. His left cheek split open, and his lips were reduced to pulp. The beating he was taking was horrendous.

The mountain man was toying with him, Rosemary realized. Nate King wasn't trying to knock Charley out. The frontiersman was whittling him down, bit by painful bit. It was cold, calculated destruction on an intensely personal scale.

Charley saw the handwriting on the chalkboard and rallied. Pausing, he set himself, his fists cocked. His breathing was irregular and his cheek and chin were streaked scarlet. One eye was pretty near swollen shut and one ear was mangled. "Damn you!" he puffed. "Damned Injun lover!"

Then Nate King did an astounding thing. He lowered his arms and said, "End this. Apologize and I'll be satisfied."

"Like hell!" Charley snarled. "I'm just getting my second wind. When I get done, even your squaw won't recognize you."

It was the wrong thing to say. Nate King raised his fists and waded in, and his onslaught was terrible to behold. Terrible, yet undeniably exciting. Rosemary had never witnessed a real fight in her life. Certainly not anything like this. A dynamic ballet of incredible brutality, so brutal it was beautiful.

King rained a withering barrage that Charley did his best to counter or avoid, but his best wasn't good enough. For maybe fifteen seconds Charley stood firm, then he retreated, blocking and slugging as he went, and each step brought new suffering, a new pain. Everyone watching knew that King could end the fight at any time with a single powerful punch, but King continued to pummel Kastner until Charley's knees buckled and his arms went limp at his sides.

King gripped Charley by the chin and bent Charley's head back so Charley could see the final blow descend. "Don't ever call my wife a squaw again," he said, and tensed to strike.

"Noooooo!"

Martha Kastner flung herself between them, shielding her man with her own body, her tear-stained face fixed on King in blatant terror.

The mountain man transformed to marble.

"Enough!" Martha wailed. "You've proven your point! Leave him be!" She threw a protective arm around her husband's shoulders. *"Please."*

Nate King's fist slowly unclenched, and his arm slowly lowered. He stared at Martha, at the bloody wreck he had made of Kastner, and at his own big hands. Finally his shoulders slumped and without comment he walked to the pilot and reclaimed his guns. "Thank you for your hospitality." He moved toward the wagons.

"Wait!" Harry Trapp requested. "I was hoping to ask you about the Sioux. You saw the same sign I did, didn't you?"

King halted in the shadows between the Conestoga and the next wagon. "It was hard to read. Your wheels had churned up the tracks. Best as I could tell, a war party of fifteen to twenty warriors crossed the trail yesterday morning, heading north."

"I couldn't tell half as much," Trapp said. "If that's the case, then they're likely on their way to their village. We have nothing to worry about."

"Maybe, maybe not," King said enigmatically. "But don't let down your guard. Bunch up during the day. Post two sentries at night. Keep your animals close and hobble them, so they can't be stolen."

"We will," Harry Trapp said. "Thanks."

The mountain man was no longer there. He had

melted into the darkness as soundlessly as he had arrived.

Rosemary succumbed to sharp disappointment. She shrugged it off with the thought that she was being foolish. King meant nothing to her, nor she to him. They were strangers passing in the night. Two ships at sea that had a chance encounter in the limitless ocean and now would sail off to different ports.

"Gosh," Eddy exclaimed, thunderstruck.

"Did you see, Pa?" Sam whispered. "Did you see what he did to Mr. Kastner?"

"How could I miss it?" Bert said in disapproval. "It was uncalled for. Charley was only speaking his mind."

Her ears burning, Rosemary spun. "I suppose you'd just sit there and do nothing if someone called me a harlot? King was defending his wife's good name. I, for one, think Charley got what he deserved and I don't care who knows it." She walked off before she used harsher language and set a bad example in front of their sons. Storming through the gap between the wagons, she stepped over a tongue and moved midway along the Conestoga. "What's gotten into Mother?" she heard Sam ask. Her husband didn't answer.

"Thank goodness that terrible man is gone!" Lucy Bateman's comment rose above the growing hubbub.

"Good riddance, I say!" bellowed Harvey Whittaker. "The nerve of that ruffian! We didn't invite him here."

Harry Trapp took command of the situation. "Calm down, all of you! Kastner brought it on himself. He's lucky to be alive. I've seen men gunned down for less." He paused. "The important thing is that the Sioux war party I was concerned about has left the area. We'll keep on taking precautions, but we can rest a lot easier now."

Rosemary distinctly recalled that King had made no such claim, but she stayed where she was, too upset to rejoin them just yet. She examined the strange emotions the mountain man had stirred in her, and tried to fathom why. No matter what the others said, she liked him. He was the kind of man she had always wished Bert would be. Strong, wise, forceful. The kind who never took guff off of anybody. The kind who wouldn't let the Pringles of the world take advantage of him.

Catching herself, Rosemary bowed her head in shame. She wasn't being fair to Bert. He did the best he could, and he loved her, heart and soul. She must forget about the mountain man. Nate King was gone from her life and she would never see him again. Squaring her shoulders, she marched back into the circle, to her waiting husband and children. "Now, then," she smiled, acting as if nothing had happened, "who would like some hot chocolate?"

Chapter Four

By now it was routine. Up before the crack of dawn, a hurried breakfast, the hustle and bustle of breaking camp, and then long, plodding hours of travel.

Rosemary had grown used to the discomforts. The blistering heat no longer affected her as much as it had initially. Swarms of insects were dismissed with a few waves of her hand. Nor did the confines of their Conestoga seem quite as cramped. She had come to regard it as a rolling oasis in the midst of the sweltering grassland, and was as protective toward it as she had once been toward the farmhouse that had been in her family for so long.

For several days after Nate King's visit the wagon train made steady progress. He wasn't spotted again, and no one mentioned him, even in passing. Charley Kastner didn't show his battered, bandaged face until late in the third day, and when he did, he boasted of how he could have won the fight if not for a lucky punch or two on King's part.

Things were back to normal.

Then, along about eleven on the fourth morning, Samson's limp returned, worse than ever. Bert applied his whip, but Samson slowed to a snail's pace and the rest of the team slowed with him. In no time the rest of the wagons were a hundred yards ahead, and the distance rapidly widened.

Harry Trapp finally noticed and trotted back down the line. He pulled in alongside of the team, dismounted, and gave the reins to Sam to hold. At his order, Bert brought the oxen to a stop and Trapp hunkered and ran his hands up and down Samson's afflicted leg. "It's not swollen, so maybe there's hope yet" was his assessment.

"Why not stop the train and let everyone rest for a day?" Bert suggested. "Samson will be right as rain tomorrow."

"I can't do that," the pilot said, adding quickly when Bert frowned, "Not here, anyway. But I'll tell you what I will do. There's a good spot to noon a couple of miles ahead. We'll stop and wait. I'll gather everyone together and ask whether they want to stay over until tomorrow, as a favor to you. We'll put it to a vote."

"That's ever so kind of you, Mr. Trapp," Rosemary said. She was positive the others would agree. She and Bert were well-liked.

"Just doing my job, ma'am." Trapp stepped into the stirrups. "Thank your lucky stars the Sioux are gone, and hurry along as best you can."

Samson was game, but he was going lame fast, and soon the wagon train was out of sight around a twisting bend of the Platte.

Rosemary experienced an unnerving twinge of fear. They were all alone, tiny ants in the immense vastness of the prairie. She felt small and insignificant, and terribly vulnerable. Suppressing her unease, she resorted to her knitting. Her sons came forward and sat close, as if to draw comfort from her presence. Bert walked beside the team, coaxing them on.

"I don't like this much, Ma," Eddy mentioned.

"We'll be fine," Rosemary assured him. But she couldn't shake a vague foreboding. Nerves, she reasoned, and chided herself for being so childish. "Let's sing a few songs," she suggested.

"I don't feel much like singing, Ma," Sam said.

"Me either," from Eddy.

Rosemary didn't press the issue. She whistled as she knitted to show she wasn't worried. Above them the blazing yellow orb rose to its zenith.

By then Samson was limping worse than ever. Bert unexpectedly brought the team to a halt and beckoned to the boys. They unhitched the stricken ox, threw a rope over him, and Sam and Eddy led him to the rear and tied him to the gate. Bert switched Methuselah from the lead pair to the slot Samson had occupied. It left Saul all alone, but it couldn't be helped.

The switch had taken a good quarter of an hour. Rosemary was glad when Bert's whip cracked and the Conestoga lurched into motion. She was eager to catch up to the others.

Sparrows warbled merrily in cottonwoods that bordered the sparkling river. Butterflies fluttered serenely amid a bed of colorful wildflowers. Shafts of brilliant sunlight bathed the surrounding grassland, lending a touch of gold to the green. So picturesque a scene, yet Rosemary wasn't fooled. The wilderness could be deceptively deadly. A lot like those snakes she had read about, coral snakes they were called, with bright yellow, red, and black rings. Snakes so spectacular, anyone who saw one and didn't know any better might be tempted to pick it up, never realizing coral snakes were among the most poisonous on the continent.

The minutes dragged by. They were moving faster, but

it took over an hour to reach the nooning site. Ahead the trail widened, and there, amid a tract of trampled grass, half a dozen campfires burned. But no one was there to tend them.

"Where is everyone?" Eddy asked.

Bewildered, Rosemary slid to the end of the seat and jumped to the ground while the Conestoga was still in motion. She ran to the nearest fire. A few of the logs had burned completely through. "They left five to ten minutes ago."

Bert brought the oxen to a halt and came over. "This doesn't make sense. Harry Trapp promised they would wait. Why did they leave without us?"

"He said they would put it to a vote," Sam said. "Maybe they voted not to."

"Maybe so," Bert said, "but they wouldn't leave their fires burning like this. It's against the pilot's own rules."

Rosemary had a sharp retort on the tip of her tongue, but she choked it down. Her opinion of the pilot plumbed new depths. What sort of man left a family of four to fend for themselves in the middle of the wilds?

"This just can't be," Bert insisted.

Eddy was gnawing on his lower lip. "What do we do now, Pa? Can we make it to the Promised Land by ourselves?"

Before Bert could answer, Sam pointed toward the river. "What's that yonder?"

A stick was embedded in the bank. It had been split at the top, and a folded sheet of paper had been wedged tight.

Sam reached it first and dutifully handed the stick to Rosemary. Her hands shaking slightly, she opened the note and held it so everyone could read the hastily scrawled contents: *Large band of hostiles sighted. Better cover five miles west. Will stay the night. Catch up or on your own. HT.*

"Good God!" Bert exclaimed.

Eddy rotated a full three hundred and sixty degrees. "I don't see any Indians, Pa."

Neither did Rosemary, but the mere notion chilled her to her marrow. "We must push on immediately," she urged, hastening toward the wagon and snagging Eddy's sleeve on the fly. "We can overtake them by nightfall if we push hard."

Bert removed his hat and mopped his brow. "The team needs water."

"And we need a godsend," Rosemary responded. Allowing the animals to drink their fill would delay them half an hour, minimum. Time they couldn't spare, not with a war party in the vicinity. "We'll water them tonight."

"They'll go faster if they're not thirsty," Bert pointed out. "Help me, boys," he said, and they rushed to the task.

Rosemary rarely asserted herself, but when she did, her husband invariably bowed to her wishes. She couldn't remember the last time he had refused. That he should do so now, of all times, when their lives were in grave peril, was beyond belief. Rather than carp, she climbed onto the Conestoga and searched the prairie in all directions.

Three oxen had been taken to drink and Bert was unhitching Isaiah, when Rosemary thought of an oversight on their part. Ducking under the canopy, she gathered up the four Pennsylvania long rifles propped in the corner and carefully climbed back out. Manufactured by German craftsmen in Lancaster, Pennsylvania, they were virtually identical to their more famous cousins, the Kentucky rifles popularized by Daniel Boone and his ilk. Each was superbly crafted, their maple stocks inlaid with silver. "You'll need these," Rosemary said.

Sam smiled as he accepted his .40-caliber. He loved to hunt and was a fair marksman. Back on the farm he had routinely provided meat for the supper pot, everything from rabbits to deer.

Eddy's rifle was shorter than the rest, and correspondingly lighter in weight and caliber. Bert had bought it at a shop in Springfield and never told Eddy it was designed for women. Bert's rifle was the biggest of the lot, a whopping .45-caliber, and capable of dropping a black bear at fifty paces.

Rosemary also passed out powder horns, ammo pouches, and patch boxes. She verified that her rifle was loaded and propped it beside her. It weighed about eight pounds, average for a Pennsylvania. In ten years she had fired it maybe ten times.

"The pistols, too," Bert requested, reaching up.

Four flintlocks were kept in a wooden box under the seat. They were heavy, unwieldy affairs, and Rosemary had to use both hands to fire one. She passed them out, and since she didn't own a belt, she borrowed one of Bert's and wedged her pistol under it.

"I'd like to see those mangy redskins make wolf bait of us now," Sam said, his rifle in one hand, his pistol in the other. "We'll send them running with their tails between their legs."

"Be careful what you wish for, boy," Bert said. "Your wish might come true."

Sam was full of vinegar and vim. "With eight guns we can hold off a horde of Indians," he stated.

Rosemary wasn't so sure. Their rifles were reliable enough out to two hundred yards and their pistols could drop a man at ten paces, but if enough hostiles rushed them at once, they would be overrun. And unlike arrows, which an Indian could unleash one after another as long as he had shafts in his quiver, their guns had to be painstakingly reloaded after each and every shot.

Bert and the boys herded the next pair of oxen toward the river, and Rosemary spent an anxious twenty minutes scouring the landscape. Several times she imagined she saw figures on horseback where there were none, illusions spawned by the harsh glare of shimmering heat. She did spy four deer in the plain to the north, and their presence reassured her that no Indians were skulking about.

Bert returned to lead Samson to the river, and the sight of the great animal barely able to put weight on its fore leg plucked at Rosemary's heartstrings. Oxen weren't necessarily bright or affectionate, but over the past several weeks she had grown somewhat attached to them. She was overjoyed when the team was once again yoked and they were ready to depart. They moved toward the point where the Oregon Trail wound to the northwest past a spur of cottonwoods.

Unexpectedly, Bert brought the team to a halt and he and the boys walked to where clods of dirt had been scoured out of the rich soil as if by a plow. Rosemary wondered why they merited so much interest. Then it dawned on her that the clods had been gouged out of the earth by horse hooves, and she jumped down for a look-see.

"I'm no tracker, but I'd guess ten or more unshod horses," Bert said, pointing at multiple overlaid tracks. "They came out of the trees, palavered a while, and rode on after the train."

"Hostiles," Eddy said. Even he knew Indians preferred unshod mounts.

"It must be that Sioux war party the mountain man warned us about," Sam said. "They didn't head back to the village like Mr. Trapp thought."

Rosemary's skin crawled. Of all the tribes, Sioux were feared the most. They resented any encroachment into their territory, and rumor had it they had taken more lives than all the other tribes combined. The Cheyenne, the Blackfeet, the Utes, they also posed a threat, but not anywhere near the same degree. The tales of Sioux atrocities were enough to frighten grown men.

"We were lucky," Bert said. "They rode off shortly before we arrived."

"The Good Lord was watching over us," Rosemary remarked. Although, truth to tell, her faith was being stretched to its limit.

"They're west of us now," Sam said, "between us and everyone else. How will we get past them?"

Bert fingered the butt of his pistol. "We'll cross that bridge when we come to it. The three of you get back into the wagon."

Eddy was gazing wide-eyed at the buffalo grass. "What if that's not all of them, Pa? What if there are more hereabouts?"

A chill descended, and Rosemary hustled her young ones to the Conestoga. They sat on either side of her, rifles at the ready. Bert hiked along next to the rear pair of oxen, as usual, but he left the whip in the wagon to free his hands so he could use his guns if he had to. To prod the team along, he swatted Solomon on the rump when need be.

"Maybe we should hide somewhere," Eddy suggested after a few minutes of travel. "Off in the trees until the hostiles are gone."

"And what if they find us, little brother?" Sam wasn't as cocky as he had been a short while before. "Fifteen or twenty bucks might be more than the four of us can handle alone. We need to rejoin the others. There's strength in numbers."

Rosemary was proud of him. Samuel was showing more signs of maturity every day. Back on the farm he and Eddy had often spatted over the silliest of trifles, much to her distress. Bert always punished them by making them do extra work, which they hated. Young people had it too easy nowadays, she had concluded. When she was young, doing chores was a given, and it was done without complaint.

"What's that?" Bert suddenly asked.

Looking up, Rosemary beheld columns of smoke coiling skyward on the horizon. Three, four, five thick coils, spaced fairly close together.

"That's about where the note said the wagon train would stop," Bert mentioned. "But why did they light such big fires?"

Sam's hawkish eyes were narrowed intently. "Maybe something else is burning."

Rosemary's chill worsened. For a long while no one spoke. The creak of the wagon, the soft rustle of the canvas, the thud of plodding oxen were the only sounds. Those, and the swish of the high grass at every gust of breeze.

Rigid with dread, Rosemary constantly scanned the prairie and the vegetation flanking the river. Every shadow hid a skulking warrior. She kept telling herself not to panic. Everything would be fine. They would catch up to the wagon train and the Sioux would fight shy of them for fear of their guns. They would make it over South Pass, out of Sioux territory, and all would be well.

"That's mighty strange," Bert remarked.

Dozens of discarded belongings littered the trail in front of them. Not just any items, but big things like a stove and a tub and a plow. Many hundreds of dollars' worth.

Bert inspected the stove. "This is from Carver's wagon. He showed it to me about a week ago. It's brand spanking new, and he was as proud as could be." Bert went to another object, and yet another. "All these are from our train."

"But why—?" Rosemary began.

"To lighten their loads, Ma," Sam said. "So their wagons can go faster. They knew the Sioux were after them."

Eddy squirmed like a worm on a hook. "Will they come after us too? Should we throw out our things?"

"Not unless we have to," Bert said. "Our whole future

51

is in our wagon. If we lose everything, it'll be hard starting over. Money doesn't grow on trees."

Rosemary appreciated his sentiment. Practically every spare cent they had was tied up in the Conestoga and its contents, and it would be a shame to cast it all aside.

"Besides," Bert had gone on, "as slow as our oxen are, if we empty the wagon we'll still go no faster than molasses in January."

Overhead the sun arced slowly westward, seeming to pace them. Rosemary tried to stay alert, but the heat sapped her energy and she grew drowsy. Twice her eyelids drooped. Twice she snapped them open again. The third time, much to her chagrin, she dozed, and awakened only when the Conestoga's wheels ground to a halt.

"We're close," Bert whispered.

An acrid scent tingled Rosemary's nose. The scent of burning wood mixed with another, subtle odor, a sickly sweet smell reminiscent of rancid fruit. The trail wound around a bend, and their view of whatever lay beyond was blocked by dense timber. Above the timber rose the columns of smoke, thinner but still there.

Bert turned. "I'll go on alone. If I holler, you're to hide as best you can. Forget our effects, forget the oxen. Your lives are all that count."

"We're a family," Rosemary said. "Where you go, we go. We've always faced things together, and we're not about to change now."

"Please, Rose. Be reasonable. I don't want any harm to come to you or the boys."

"And we don't want any harm to come to you, so we're even," Rosemary said. "It's not open to debate, Bertram. It's all or none, do or die." Sam's hand found hers and squeezed, and at that moment he looked prouder of her than he'd ever been. So did Bert, but he hesitated nonetheless until Rosemary called out, "Get going, there!" and smacked Solomon and Isaiah with the butt of her rifle.

The sickly sweet smell grew stronger. Black specks high in the sky caught Rosemary's eye. Buzzards, their long black wings spread wide, were circling in graceful spirals. "Lord help us," she breathed.

Yard by yard the oxen plodded forward. The lead animals snorted and bobbed their huge heads, and the entire team slowed of their own accord.

Bert let them set their own pace. He was riveted to the horrifying spectacle unfolding ahead, a scene of nightmare made real.

The wagon train had been attacked. From the look of things, it happened while they were beginning to wheel into a circle. The Sioux had struck hard and fast, killing mules as well as people. Five wagons had been stopped in their tracks, their teams riddled with arrows. The mules lay dead in their harness, tongues lolling, eyes glassy, rimmed by overlapping pools of drying blood.

The human corpses shocked Rosemary more. Men, women, and children were sprawled like pale leafs in a hurricane. Some bristled with feathered shafts. Others had been slashed with knives or gouged with tomahawks. Tom Weaver was on his back, half his skull crushed in. Mrs. Weaver had taken a lance in her torso. Old Man Farnum's neck was connected to his body by a shred of flesh. Two arrows had caught Charley Kastner in the back as he fled toward the trees, and his bragging days were over. He had run off leaving his wife and child behind, and they were still in their wagon—or what was left of them—locked arm in arm, their bodies charred almost beyond recognition.

Five wagons. Twenty-three people. And not a dead Indian anywhere. Rosemary put a hand to her mouth and shuddered. "We should bury these poor souls."

"I don't see Harry Trapp anywhere," Bert said. "And three of the wagons are missing. The Crane family, the Pendergast, and the Garveys."

"With the hostiles right after them," Sam said. He had

hopped down and was roving among the slain. "Notice anything peculiar, Pa?"

Bert looked, but not too closely, and shook his head.

For a fifteen-year-old, Sam was as sharp as broken glass. "None of them have been scalped. None have been mutilated."

"That means the Sioux will be back after they finish with the rest. We have to get clear of this area or we're goners."

"Where can we go?" Rosemary asked. Other than off across the prairie, where they were bound to be caught. Their oxen couldn't outdistance Indian ponies.

Her husband was thinking the same thing. "We're trapped like flies on flypaper," he growled. "The best we can do is pick a spot to make our stand and take as many of them with us as we can."

Eddy sidled next to Rosemary. "I don't want to die, Ma."

Sam was scratching his hairless chin. "Maybe we don't have to. Maybe we can outfox these red devils."

Bert's interest was piqued. "How, son?"

"That bend we passed, all that thick timber. What if we hide out in it? Ride our wagon far enough into the trees, maybe the Sioux won't notice. Sooner or later they'll leave and we can go on our own way."

"Hiding is a good idea, son," Bert said, "but I'll go you one better. We have enough grub to last us weeks. We'll stay hidden until the next wagon train comes along and hook up with them."

"It's late in the season, remember?" Rosemary noted. "There might not be another train this year."

"There was talk in Independence of another leaving in a week or two. Southerners, mostly, overdue from the Carolinas and Georgia. The clerk at the general store was hoping he had enough stock on hand to meet their needs."

Sam smiled. "Then we won't be stuck here long, Pa."

It was an iffy proposition, Rosemary mused, but what other choice did they have? "We need to hurry. The hostiles might return at any minute."

Bert ran to the lead ox and guided the team in a semicircle to bring the Conestoga around. The big brutes moved as swiftly as they could, but to Rosemary they were worse than turtles. She chafed at their shuffling pace and lent Bert a hand. Sam and Eddy were watching the trail.

"Rose, I've got something I want to say," Bert quietly mentioned as the wagon completed its turn.

"Then say it." Rosemary assumed it pertained to the Sioux and their prospects of survival.

"I love you, Rose. With all my heart and soul. Remember that, will you?"

Rosemary was taken aback, yet pleased beyond measure. He rarely mentioned how he felt about her. "I love you, too, Bertram." Intuition enlightened her on why he was suddenly so outspoken, and she added, "Don't even think of dying on me. I aim to live to a ripe old age with you by my side."

Bert acted as if he hadn't heard her. "It's all my fault, Rose. We never should have left Missouri. Never should have sold the farm."

"You did what you thought best. And I went along with it." Rosemary gently brushed his hand with her fingertips. "Only shirkers give up, and the Spencers aren't shirkers."

Bert smiled, and pointed the oxen toward the bend.

Slowing to walk beside her sons, Rosemary commented, "We'll get out of this fix. Wait and see."

"Whatever you say, Ma," Sam said, his tone implying he didn't share her confidence.

Eddy had a question. "Ever wondered what it's like to die, Ma?"

"You're too young to be thinking about something so

ridiculous," Rosemary said with feigned lightheartedness. "Trust me. You'll outlive all of us."

Glancing westward, Sam stopped, his hand rising to shield his eyes. "Dust," he announced. "A mile off, maybe closer."

As swiftly as they could, they drove the oxen around the bend and into the timber, Bert guiding the lead ox by hand. The boys helped by smacking any animal that showed the least little reluctance. The tree trunks were closely spaced, and threading the Conestoga through them was a feat in itself. They halted a stone's throw from the Platte. Bert and the boys did what they could to conceal their tracks and to restore the crushed vegetation to some semblance of normal. Then the four of them hastily chopped a dozen limbs and leaned them against the wagon to camouflage it. That done, they huddled by the front wheel. They did not have long to wait.

Seconds later, yipping like coyotes, painted Sioux warriors came galloping down the Oregon Trail.

Chapter Five

Rosemary Spencer's insides congealed into a block of ice. *Sioux warriors!* The most fierce on the plains! Twelve had appeared seventy yards away, whooping and howling like banshees. They rode bareback yet with supreme skill, many of their mounts bearing painted symbols she did not know how to decipher. One horse had a red disk on its side; another bore long horizontal lines. Others had stripes on either their right or left legs. Similar but smaller symbols were painted on many of the warriors.

In a cloud of dust the Sioux reined up and leaped down. Most were young, in their twenties, Rosemary reckoned. Spreading out, they went from body to body.

Rosemary had always envisioned the Sioux as hideous primitives, more beastlike than human, but they were nothing of the sort. They were ordinary men, the majority not all that tall. Their bodies were on the stocky side, and while none had bulging sinews as she had imagined, they were powerfully built. Buckskin shirts and leggings was their typical attire, and their clothes, like their bodies and their animals, were adorned with mysterious symbols. Their hair was worn long, some braided, some not.

Something else caught Rosemary's interest. Almost all the warriors wore eagle feathers in their hair, not large war bonnets, as a traveling salesman once claimed the plains tribes favored. One or two feathers at most, except in the case of older warriors, who wore three. And the odd thing about it was, the feathers were worn at all different angles. Some feathers pointed upward, some were horizontal, others pointed down. There had to be some significance as to why, but it eluded Rosemary.

"Ma, look!" Eddy whispered.

One of the warriors had straddled Tom Weaver and jerked Weaver's head back.

Drawing a knife, the Sioux slashed twice, raised his trophy aloft, and howled.

Several warriors converged on Charley Kastner. They rolled him over, stripped him naked, and proceeded to whittle on him as if he were a pasty block of wood. They cut off his nose, sliced off his ears. They gouged out his eyes, removed his tongue. They mutilated him low down. And all the while they talked and laughed as if it were a great joke.

"I think I'm going to be sick," Eddy said. Turning toward the wagon, he doubled over.

Rosemary tore her gaze from the unspeakable deeds being committed and placed a hand on his shoulder. "Do it quietly, if you must," she whispered. "If they hear us, we're done for."

"They're not touching the women or the children," Sam observed.

It was true. The warriors were butchering only men. And there seemed to be some method to their madness. They made a point of selecting certain men and avoiding others. When two younger warriors argued hotly over

58

Join the Western Book Club and GET 4 FREE* BOOKS NOW!
A $19.96 VALUE!

— Yes! I want to subscribe — to the Western Book Club.

Please send me my **4 FREE* BOOKS**. I have enclosed $2.00 for shipping/handling. Each month I'll receive the four newest Leisure Western selections to preview for 10 days. If I decide to keep them, I will pay the Special Members Only discounted price of just $3.36 each, a total of $13.44, plus $2.00 shipping/handling ($22.30 US in Canada). This is a **SAVINGS OF AT LEAST $6.00** off the bookstore price. There is no minimum number of books I must buy, and I may cancel the program at any time. In any case, the **4 FREE* BOOKS** are mine to keep.

*In Canada, add $5.00 shipping/handling per order for the first shipment. For all future shipments to Canada, the cost of membership is $22.30 US, which includes shipping and handling.
(All payments must be made in US dollars.)

NAME: _____

ADDRESS: _____

CITY: _____ STATE: _____

COUNTRY: _____ ZIP: _____

TELEPHONE: _____

E-MAIL: _____

SIGNATURE: _____

the same body, the oldest warrior approached and silenced them with a gesture. He addressed each in turn, then quizzed some of their companions. His mind made up, he pointed at one of the two disputants, who grinned, yanked out a knife, and bent to his grisly handiwork. The other warrior walked off, scowling.

To Rosemary it was apparent that the pair had been arguing over who got to carve the dead man up. Maybe it had something to do with which one of them had slain him. That would make sense. Their dispute was so childish, so like the squabbles her sons were prone to, it impressed on her the remarkable fact that for all their ferocity and savage reputation the Sioux were no different from her own kind. They were red men, but men nonetheless. The revelation tempered her fear. She was right to be scared of them. Any sane person would. But her unreasoning terror evaporated.

Bert was ashen, his face slick with sweat. Sam was riveted to the tableau, drinking in every detail with the intense interest of a scholar poring over a long-lost volume of forgotten lore. Eddy couldn't stand to watch.

Rosemary was the same, although she looked up now and then. She was thinking about Harry Trapp and the three missing families and wondering if they had made it safely away. She doubted it. The Sioux had wiped them out, then come back to finish up. She hoped they would soon end their butchery and leave, but to her consternation they were in no great hurry. The mutilation of the men done, they turned to the women.

Rosemary gasped as a stocky warrior stood over Mrs. Pendergast, bloody knife poised. Instead of scalping her, he plucked at her dress, puzzled by its texture. Bending lower, he tried to remove her necklace. The clasp yielded its secret, and he straightened, smiling broadly, and slid his prize into a pouch.

One of the Sioux was standing next to Charley Kastner's wife, Martha. His expression was sad, and when he touched her hair, he did so gently, almost regretfully. Then he respectfully folded her arms across her bosom.

The more Rosemary saw, the more food for thought she had. Her ears perked at the drum of more hooves, and six more warriors trotted onto the scene. All were waving fresh scalps, and one wore Harry Trapp's short-brimmed black hat. The oldest warrior consulted with them, and at a yell from him, the entire war party swung astride their war horses and rode north.

Rosemary stayed rooted in place until the last of the retreating figures was lost to view. Then she let out a breath and said softly, "They're gone! We're safe at last!"

Bert lowered his rifle. "Are we?" he said skeptically. "I wouldn't take anything for granted, not unless we want to wind up like them." He nodded toward the remains of their unfortunate former traveling companions.

Sam dashed to a nearby tree, leaned his rifle against it, and leaped straight up. Catching hold of a low limb, he climbed with the agility of a squirrel and was soon thirty feet up, shielding his eyes from the sun.

"What are you doing?" Rosemary inquired, concerned that the Sioux might spot him.

"Making darned sure those redskins are leaving." Sam watched awhile, then descended to report, "They're out of sight, and I didn't see any others anywhere."

"The Lord preserved us," Rosemary said, and was annoyed when Bert frowned. She wondered why she hadn't noticed his lack of faith before. Was it because it had never been put to the test? "Who would like some water?" she asked. Her throat was parched, her mouth so dry it hurt to swallow.

It turned out they all would. They took turns, treating themselves to a full dipper from the water keg on the other side of the Conestoga.

Eddy was uncharacteristically subdued. When they moved into the shade and sat, he put an arm around her and leaned his head on her shoulder. "What those Indians did was awful, Ma. Just plain awful."

"Try not to dwell on it," Rosemary said, which was easier suggested than done. She wouldn't be surprised if they all suffered nightmares for years to come. She knew she would, as surely as she was sitting there.

For once Bert didn't produce his pipe. "I won't try to deceive you," he began. "We're in a tight fix. We're stranded in Sioux country, and there's no telling how long we'll be here. We can't fire our guns, we can't build a fire."

"Not even to cook with?" Rosemary said.

"And have the Sioux see the smoke?" Bert rejoined. "Maybe in four or five days, once we're absolutely certain they're long gone. But it will have to be a small fire, and we'll keep a bucket of water handy to douse it fast if we have to."

"I can go for help, Pa," Sam volunteered. "I'm right handy at living off the land. I'll head east until I meet up with the next train, and I'll ask some of them to hurry on ahead and stay with us until the train gets here."

"A noble notion," Bert said, "but it's best if we stick together. You and I must take turns standing guard at night. And if we're attacked, well . . ." He dabbed at his slick face with a sleeve.

Rosemary shifted. "What about poor Mrs. Kastner and the rest?"

"What about them?"

"Shouldn't we do the decent thing and bury them?"

"There are too many. It would take forever. And we'd be out in the open, where the hostiles are more apt to catch sight of us." Bert shook his head. "No, we have to leave the bodies where they are."

"That's not very Christian," Rosemary criticized. She was beginning to think she had never truly known him.

"But it's for the best," Bert stressed, "unless you want to end up just like them."

David Thompson

"Of course not." But Rosemary didn't like it, she didn't like it one bit. Women and children being left to rot in the sun, or to be devoured by scavengers. Some of those children were under five years old, sweet innocents too soon deprived of life and promise. She couldn't see the harm in burying them, at the very least.

Bert had more to say. "We'll cut more branches to better conceal the wagon. Then we'll picket the oxen. Twice a day we'll cut grass and feed them, but we can't risk taking them out onto the plain to graze. We couldn't get them back in time if the Sioux happen by."

"I hate the Sioux," Eddy said softly. "Hate them, hate them, hate them."

Bert tried to bolster their spirits. "It could be worse. We have plenty of water, plenty of supplies. We can hold out here a good long while."

"Unless the Indians get us," Eddy said.

"They won't." Rosemary gave him a heartfelt hug. "I won't let them harm a hair on your head."

Eddy grinned, but fear lurked deep in his youthful eyes, and when he gazed out across the prairie, he shivered ever so slightly.

A busy hour ensued. Bert unhitched the oxen and picketed them on the far side of a thicket within short walking distance of the river. Sam chopped enough leafy branches to conceal their vehicle from bottom to top. It wouldn't withstand a close scrutiny but should suffice against a casual glance.

By late afternoon twenty vultures were feasting royally on the remains of their friends. Every few minutes more winged in from all points of the compass. How the buzzards knew where to come, Rosemary had no idea. Instinct, maybe.

Rosemary refrained from looking. She couldn't stand the sight. Toward sunset, canine yowls pealed across the prairie, and by twilight coyotes were gathering. With throaty snarls and snaps of their bared teeth, they drove off the buzzards. No sooner had the harbingers of death risen flapping into the sky than their four-legged scavenging brethren tore into the corpses, ripping and rending and gulping in an orgy of feral excess.

Seated on the opposite side of the Conestoga so as not to have the abominable images seared into her memory, Rosemary heard the crunch of iron teeth on bone. Not loud, not at that distance, but loud enough to roil her stomach and induce a queasy feeling. Yesterday she had shared pleasantries with many of those people; now she was sitting there like a bump on a log while they were being eaten.

Enough was enough. Rising, Rosemary took her rifle and crept toward the site of the massacre. Bert was off cutting grass. Sam was filling the water keg. The stress had been to much for Eddy, and he was napping in the Conestoga. So no one would try to stop her.

The smell of blood and overripe bodies made Rosemary gag. Ten coyotes were eating, and none were disposed to relinquish their meal. Overhead the buzzards circled, although not for long. Once night fell, they would fly off to roost, then return at first light to gorge on whatever the coyotes left.

The wagons were smoldering ruins. Only one still blazed, what little was left of it. From it Rosemary selected a burning brand. The coyotes eyed her warily, their normally timid dispositions eclipsed by their hunger. She moved toward the nearest, and they growled menacingly. Swinging the brand from side to side, she continued to advance.

The coyotes retreated, but they did not go far. Ears pricked, tongues lolling, they stood and stared, implicitly challenging her to drive them off.

Rosemary regarded them coolly. Her brand would not burn forever. She must act quickly and decisively. On an impulse she charged the largest coyote. It skipped backward, wary of the flame, but it wasn't quite fast enough, and with a bound Rosemary plunged the brand into its face. Uttering a shrill cry, the large coyote wheeled and fled, and with him went the rest.

Rosemary turned. There wasn't much time. The sun had set, and soon it would be too dark to dig. She stepped toward a frail form lying near its mother and leaned down to grasp a tiny hand. Her muscles locked, and she couldn't bring herself to move. The face below hers wasn't that of the small girl she remembered. The eyes were gone, popped from their sockets by a buzzard's expert beak, and the girl's lips and other soft parts had been chewed by a coyote. The child's neck was a stringy cavity, the flesh lacerated into thin strips.

Sudden dizziness caused Rosemary to shuffle sideways and sink to her knees. She felt sick, terribly sick, and she closed her eyes and groaned in an agony of despair. Little Cecilia! So lively! So full of glee! Now a ravaged bundle of soon-to-be-rotting flesh.

Rosemary's faith wavered. Why had God permitted the atrocity? What had those people done to justify their ugly ends? Her parson would say all men and women were born in sin and deserved whatever evil befell them. Yet even so, were the sins of the emigrants so vile they merited a harvest of sheer savagery? What had little Cecilia ever done that her life should be so callously extinguished?

Choking down bitter bile, Rosemary leaned on her rifle and gathered her thoughts. She couldn't bring herself to touch the girl, let alone bury her. It had been wrong to sneak off. She must return to the Conestoga before her loved ones discovered she was missing.

The thud of hooves fell on Rosemary's ears. But were they really hooves? She strained to hear them again and was about convinced her rattled nerves were to blame when she heard a couple more. A horse, or two, was moving at a slow walk and stopping every few yards, somewhere to the west. *More Sioux!* Rosemary deduced, and flew across the slaughter ground to the edge of the timber. Barreling into the undergrowth, breathless with apprehension, she crouched low.

Night had fallen with alarming rapidity, the shadows spreading and blending into a veil of darkness so complete that Rosemary couldn't see the end of her rifle when she wedged it to her shoulder. She glanced toward the Conestoga, invisible amid the trees. Only seventy yards away, yet it might as well be on the moon. She would make too much noise trying to reach it, so for the time being she was content to sit tight and wait for the Sioux to give their presence away.

Crickets began chirping. Along the river frogs started croaking. An owl hooted several times and was answered by another.

But were they owls? Rosemary remembered being told Indians were adept at imitating animal sounds, especially birds, to communicate back and forth. With her thumb on her rifle's hammer, she eased up high enough to sweep her vicinity for telltale motion. She no longer heard the dull hoofbeats. It could be the warriors had dismounted. It could be they knew right where she was, and they were closing in at that very moment.

An impulse to bolt to the Conestoga seized her, but Rosemary ignored it. She would end up leading the savages right to her family.

A whisper of sound caught Rosemary's breath in her throat. Was it the wind, or someone moving? She couldn't see anyone, but she had the impression that unseen eyes were upon her. Desperate for a target, she swung her rifle from right to left, praying one of the warriors would be careless. She should have known better. They were Sioux. They could move like ghosts. She strained until her eyes hurt, but the darkness mocked her.

The suspense began to tell. Rosemary wanted out of there, wanted with all her heart and soul to whirl and run, but her love for her family smothered her fear. Not completely. She was quaking inside, but her arms were steady and her finger was curled flat around the trigger. *Where are you?* she mentally screamed. If only they would show themselves!

The owl hooted again, a lot closer than before, so close Rosemary jumped and pivoted. An inky tangle hid the source. Bird or man? That was the question. Her life hinged on the answer.

Then it happened.

Behind her a twig crunched. Rosemary spun and saw a vague shape detach itself from a cluster of cottonwoods and glide soundlessly toward her. How the warrior had gotten behind her was a mystery, but he had, and odds were that other Sioux were converging and would overwhelm her at any moment.

She would go down fighting, Rosemary resolved. She had never thought of herself as particularly brave, but she refused to go meekly into eternity. She refused to turn the other cheek, not after what the Sioux had done.

Rosemary sighted down the rifle, but the bead was indistinguishable from the darkness. The best she could do was point the muzzle at the center of the advancing figure and hope she scored. Ever so slowly, she thumbed back the hammer. Another ten feet and she would fire. The Sioux would be so close, she couldn't miss.

Without warning, arms encircled Rosemary from the rear and held her tightly. Steely muscles lifted her bodily into the air and she was swung partway around. Warm breath fanned her left ear. "Don't shoot. It's your son."

Hearing English shocked her. Rosemary felt the scrape of a beard on her neck. "Nate, is that you?"

"None other," the mountain man said, his arms loosening.

The vague figure had resolved itself into a silhouette of Sam. "Ma?" he whispered urgently. "Is that you?"

Nate King answered in her stead. "If it wasn't her, boy,

you'd be dead. You're old enough to know not to pull such a boneheaded stunt."

Sam hurried up. "Mr. King? Where did you come from? And Ma, what the dickens are you doing out here by your lonesome? Pa's fit to be tied. He's off searching for you too."

"Is that your wagon yonder, I take it?" In the dark the mountain man loomed larger than ever. "You and your mother go on back."

"You can see it in this pitch?" Rosemary marveled. She knew exactly where the Conestoga was, yet she couldn't tell it was there.

"I'll fetch my horse and be with you shortly." King's huge form moved off. "Keep your eyes skinned. There's a griz in the area. The smell of blood brought him in, and he'll be edgy."

A *grizzly?* Rosemary's heart leaped to her throat. Of all the beasts inhabiting the wilds, none were more formidable. They were monsters, enormous slabs of muscle and bone impossibly hard to kill. Four-legged eating machines, with teeth and claws as long as her fingers and strength enough to crush a person's skull with a single swipe of a gigantic paw. "How close is it?" she whispered, but Nate King was out of earshot.

Sam touched her arm. "Come on, Ma." His tone betrayed his nervousness. "Stick close and try not to make much noise."

Shoulder to shoulder, they carefully picked their way through the vegetation. Rosemary tried to move as quietly as her son, but her dress kept snagging on brush and twice she stepped on dry twigs that cracked underfoot.

"Pa thought maybe the Sioux had taken you," Sam whispered. "I never saw him so upset in all my born days."

"Did your brother go with him?"

"No, Ed's still asleep in the wagon. We didn't want to leave him alone, but we didn't want to wake him, either."

Rosemary rarely swore, but she did so now—inwardly, at herself, for being such a jackass. She should never have gone off alone. Her carelessness had put her family in greater peril than ever.

Suddenly a scream rent the night, a high-pitched wail of mortal terror.

"Eddy!" Sam cried, and bolted for the Conestoga.

Rosemary tried to keep up, but he was twice as fast and had a knack for avoiding obstacles. When she got there he was at the rear of the Conestoga, and Eddy was clinging to him and crying. "What is it? What's the matter?" she demanded as her youngest flung himself at her.

"He woke up and no one was here. It scared him," Sam said.

A constriction in her throat, Rosemary hugged Eddy close. "It's all right, son. You're safe now."

Between sobs the boy choked out, "It was you I was worried about! Don't ever leave me alone again." His thin arms wrapped tighter and he sobbed uncontrollably.

Tears moistened Rosemary's eyes. His fear, his anguish, were her fault. She could feel his heart hammering wildly, and she wanted to kick herself. "We're here now, and we won't leave you. I promise."

"Something's coming, Ma."

Rosemary looked up. Sam was pointing to the east. Something big was out there, and for a moment she thought it must be Nate King on horseback. Then she remembered that the mountain man had gone off to the west, not the east. She realized what the thing must be an instant before a rumbling growl proved her right. Her own heart hammering wildly, she backed against the Conestoga.

"The grizzly!" Sam blurted, his rifle leaping to his shoulder.

"No!" Rosemary cried. In the dark he might miss or merely wound it, and wounded bears were twice as dangerous. "Don't do anything! Maybe it will leave us be!"

Sam retreated next to her. "What if it doesn't?"

Lord, but the beast was enormous! Rosemary clutched Eddy to her as the grizzly lumbered near enough for them to distinguish its massive head and the huge hump between its mountainous shoulders. Its eyes glittered demonically in the starlight, and when its mouth yawned wide to emit another growl, so did its long teeth.

"I should shoot, Ma! I should shoot!" Panic tinged Sam's voice.

"You'll do no such thing!" Rosemary directed. The grizzly wasn't more than twenty feet away, and it would be on them before they could flee. She swore she felt its hot, fetid breath on her face, and could smell its rank odor.

Eddy had stopped crying and was shaking instead, shaking so violently Rosemary was afraid it would trigger an attack. "Be still," she whispered. "We'll be fine so long as we don't make any sudden moves." But would they? The grizzly stood there staring and rasping like a bellows.

Then the undergrowth north of them crackled, and out of the night hurtled Bert. He saw them, saw the bear, and sidled forward, putting himself between them and the meat-eater. "If it charges, run. I'll try to stop it," he whispered.

The grizzly growled and took a short step. Nostrils flaring, it sniffed loudly more than half a dozen times.

Rosemary braced for a rush. She was certain the bear had caught the scent of their provisions in the wagon. But the grizzly wheeled and departed the way it had come, melting into the darkness like a shadow into shade. How an animal so immense could move so silently was beyond her.

Bert turned, the silvertip already forgotten. "Where the blazes did you get to, Rose?" he demanded. "I was worried half to death. You could have gotten some of us killed, traipsing off like that."

Warm words of greeting died on Rosemary's tongue. His anger was justified, but it made her mad he was criticizing her instead of taking her into his arms. "I went to bury the dead children."

"After I'd advised against it?" Bert was incredulous.

"Would you feel the same if they were our boys?" Rosemary asked. "I only did what I'd want others to do for us."

Their argument was cut short by an almost human squeal of torment from near the Platte River. It was followed by a thunderous roar and a terrible thrashing that ended with the sickeningly loud crunch of bone.

Bert stiffened and spun. "The grizzly! It's after our oxen!" And he was off, sprinting madly to the rescue.

Chapter Six

"Bertram, no!" Rosemary Spencer shouted, but her husband failed to heed and plunged into the undergrowth. She took a step after him, felt her youngest's legs flop against her own, and realized she was still holding Eddy. Shoving him at Sam, she commanded, "Climb in the wagon and stay there!"

"But Ma!" Sam protested.

"But nothing!" Grasping her rifle in both hands, Rosemary ran toward the river—toward the thicket, out of which came the most horrifying racket she had ever heard. The oxen were making sounds she couldn't conceive oxen capable of—lowing shrieks and almost-human screams that mingled with the roars and snarls of their attacker.

Rosemary ran flat out. She admired her husband's courage in trying to save the team, but he was one man against a grizzly, and she was scared to death of losing him. Out of nowhere hooves pounded, and an arm corded with rock-hard muscle looped around her waist. She was swung up in front of the rider, and twisting, she found herself nose-to-nose with Nate King.

"Forget your animals," the mountain man advised. "There's nothing you can do."

"My husband went to help them!" Rosemary cried, pointing.

"Damn." Nate King swung her to the ground, hollered, "Get back to your wagon!" and was off like a shot, his legs slapping the sides of his big bay.

Rosemary rotated, intending to do as he wanted, but the blast of a rifle and a roar that could shatter mountains sent her flying in the frontiersman's wake. There was another shot, this time the crack of a pistol, and a scream that was definitely human.

"Bert!" Rosemary raced around a tree trunk and almost collided with an onrushing behemoth. She shrieked, thinking it was the grizzly. But it was one of the oxen, fleeing in panic. Behind it was another, and yet a third. They weren't about to stop or swerve aside. She dodged behind a trunk and pressed flat against it as the earth under her shook and the air filled with dust and the musk of bovine sweat.

Just then a second rifle boomed, the loudest shot yet. Nate King's Hawken, Rosemary figured, and flung herself into the thicket. She heard loud splashing and a series of guttural grunts and growls, fading rapidly. A few more strides and she reached the spot where the team had been picketed.

"No!" Rosemary wailed, drawing up short.

Two oxen were down, one with its head bent at an unnatural angle, the other with its neck ripped wide and dark gashes on its shoulders and forelegs. But it wasn't the stricken oxen that cleaved her heart and petrified her soul. It was the spread-eagle shape on the riverbank.

"Bertram!"

Nate King was on one knee beside her husband, scanning the opposite shore while holding on to the reins of his skittish bay. "We have to get him out of here," he said. "The griz dragged off one of your oxen, but it's wounded and might come back."

Rosemary knelt next to Bert and lifted his head into her lap. Only then did she see what the bear had done to his upper chest and left side. "My God!"

Nate King thrust his Hawken at her. "You carry this and bring my horse. I'll carry your man." With an ease that belied Bert's one hundred and eighty pounds, the mountain man scooped her husband into his arms. Moving sideways so he could keep one eye on the other side of the Platte, King hastened into the trees at a pace she was hard-pressed to keep up with without running.

"Bert. Oh, Bert," Rosemary said softly.

"He put two balls into the bear, but they weren't enough. It was about to finish him off when I added another. I tried to go for a lung shot, but even that wasn't enough."

"Why didn't you shoot at its head?" Rosemary's father had told her the best hunters always went for a head shot.

"A grizzly's skull is too thick," King responded. "Most balls just graze off."

"Bert has to live." Rosemary voiced her innermost fear aloud. "He has to."

The mountain man was silent. Soon the Conestoga hove out of the gloom and a pair of pale faces peered down at them over the seat.

"Ma?" Eddy said. "Is that Pa he's carrying?"

Sam rose and hooked a leg over the seat, about to jump down. "What happened? Is Pa hurt bad?"

"We need blankets," Nate King said, and as Sam ducked back into the wagon, he carefully lowered Bert to the grass. "We'll also need bandages," he told Rosemary. "It's a risk, but we'll have to start a fire, too, to

David Thompson

boil water. If we don't clean his wounds, infection can set in. Hurry. Every second counts."

The next several minutes were a whirlwind of activity. Eddy gathered dry wood.

Sam procured several blankets. Rosemary found her medicine kit and a roll of clean cotton cloth.

Nate King started the fire himself, using a fire steel and flint taken from his large leather pouch. Once the flames were high enough, he hunkered to examine Bert.

So did Rosemary. One look, and the blood drained from her face and neck like water down a sink. Sam gasped and recoiled a step. Eddy whimpered like a puppy and covered his eyes with both hands.

The grizzly's claws had shattered half of Bert's rib cage and caved in half his sternum. Jagged spear-points of bone jutted from the flesh on his upper chest and low down at his hip. Out of a cavity the size of a melon flowed rivulets of blood. Several of Bert's internal organs were visible.

"No!" Sam declared. "Please, no!"

Rosemary turned away, unable to endure the sight. Her head swam and the world around her blurred, and she thought she would faint. *Lord in heaven!* She couldn't lose Bertram! She just couldn't! For all his flaws she loved him dearly, and life without him was unthinkable.

"Do something, Ma," Sam pleaded. "There must be something you can do."

Nate King sat back, bowed his chin a moment, then looked at her oldest. "I'm sorry, boy. There's no way we can patch up a hole that big. The best we can do is make him comfortable." He unfolded another blanket and gently laid it over Bert, chin high, hiding the bear's gruesome handiwork.

Sam tottered as if drunk, then dropped his rifle and threw himself onto his knees.

"Not like this!" he bawled. "Pa! Can you hear me?

Please don't die on us! *Please!*" He placed a hand on his father's shoulder, his lips quivering, tears dampening his cheeks.

Rosemary's dizzy sensation faded. Marshaling her energy, she turned toward Eddy. He was cringing against the rear wheel, a portrait in misery. She wrapped her arm around him and he collapsed, too weak to stand on his own. "I know it's hard, but we must hold ourselves together," she said, smoothing his hair. "We must be brave. We must be strong."

"Is that you, Rose?"

At the croaked question all eyes fell on Bert. His eyes were open, but his eyelids were fluttering like a butterfly's wings. One hand rose feebly, bulging against the blanket, then flopped back down.

"I feel so strange, Rose. So weak. So very weak."

Rosemary was on her knees in a twinkling, Sam on her left, Eddy on her right. "We're here, Bertram," she said tenderly. "All of us are here."

"Why is it so dark?" Bert's eyelids had stopped fluttering, and he sluggishly shifted his head from side to side. "I can't see a thing. We should get a fire going." He attempted to sit up but couldn't. "Where are you? Where are the boys?"

Sliding a hand under the blanket, Rosemary clasped his cold fingers and squeezed. "We're right beside you," she said huskily.

New horror spread across Bert's features. "The bear! You've got to watch out for that bear!"

"It's gone, dearest," Rosemary said, choking out the words. Teardrops rained from her eyes, and her nose was clogged. "We're safe now."

"I drove it off? Good." Bert relaxed and grinned. "For a minute there I was afraid we were all goners."

"Pa?" Eddy said, pushing the blanket partway aside so he could hold his father's wrist. "It's me, Ed. Please don't die on us, Pa. We need you. I don't know what I'd do without you."

"Who said anything about dying?" Bert said, and gave a tiny start. "What's that heat I feel? A fire? Why can't I see it? Why can't I see any of—" His voice broke. "Oh. Oh, my Lord."

His other hand moved, and Rosemary could tell he was trying to gauge the full extent of his injuries. Reaching across, she held his wrist gently but firmly and said in a strangled whisper, "Don't, Bertram. You don't want to know."

"I don't?" Bert's next words were barely audible. "Not here. Not now. Not like this."

No one said anything. Sam stepped around to the other side and held his father's other hand in both of his, tears dripping from his chin.

Rosemary tried to adopt a brave front for the benefit of her sons. She resisted a rising wave of despair, the heartache well-nigh unbearable. Memories of her years with Bert flashed unbidden across her mind's eye: their awkward courtship, the heat of their newlywed passion, the birth of their first son, the incomparable joy of holding a newborn in her arms, Edward's birth, the constant struggle to keep the farm afloat. There had been rough times, sure, but the good far outweighed the bad. So many wonderful years together! All the happiness they had shared! Groaning, she bowed her head.

"Sweet Bert," Rosemary said, and shuddered. At any moment their days together would end and she would be cast adrift with two boys under her wing. On the farm their prospects would have been difficult enough. Here in the wilderness they were considerably bleaker. Their oxen were dead or had been run off. They might need to abandon all their worldly possessions. The area was crawling with savages, a grizzly was on the prowl, and they were hundreds of miles from the nearest town or settlement. How could it get any worse?

Bert coughed several times and a drop of blood formed at a corner of his mouth. "We need to talk, Rose."

Rosemary gazed down on the features she knew as well as her own, her love for him welling to the surface. "Be still, my darling. Talking will only make you worse."

"This is too important," Bert said. "I realize I'm done for. I'm as close to Oregon as I'll ever get, and there are things I must tell you." His fingers entwined with hers. "The poke containing all the money we have left is hidden in our chest of drawers. It's not a lot. Two hundred and forty-seven dollars. But it should tide you over your first year in the Promised Land."

"You want us to go on?" Rosemary said. To her way of thinking it was smarter to turn back. She could get a job in Independence or some other town and scrimp and save until she had enough to buy property. Another small farm would be nice. Or, failing that, a place on the outskirts with a few acres the boys could roam.

"Oregon is our dream, Rose. A new life, a better life, with more land and more opportunity. If you give up, the dream dies. Don't let that happen."

"Bert, I'm just one woman—"

"A strong woman. The strongest I ever met. All these years, who was it who always encouraged me not to give up hope? Who bolstered my spirits when they were low? Who was always there for me when I needed her?" Bert's words were coming faster, and he sucked in a deep breath at the end of every statement and question. "I'm not saying it won't be a challenge. I'm not saying there won't be years of struggle. But since when has that ever fazed you?" His mouth curled in a lopsided smile. "That time the locusts pretty near ate all our crops, who was it rolled up her sleeves and drug me out into the fields to salvage what we could? When the drought hit, who was right beside me digging a new well?"

"We've always worked well together," Rosemary said proudly. "Don't sell yourself short." She had always been in awe of his raw physical power and endurance. Men, in general, she had learned, were blessed with more strength and stamina than women. An oversight on the Almighty's part, if ever there was one.

Bert had more to impart. "You've got Sam. You've got Ed. And you can always hire a laborer, if need be. So don't give up on my account. I thought you loved me more than that."

"Bertram," Rosemary said, her cheeks burning with more than tears, "I've never loved anyone as much as I do you."

"Then prove it, Rose. Make our dream come true. Go to Oregon, stake a claim, and start over. If you don't, the ordeal we've gone through will have been for nothing." Bert's grip became a vise. "If you don't, I'll have died in vain."

Rosemary was torn between devotion and common sense. The last thing she wanted was to let Bert down, but he was asking the impossible. There were limits to what she could do. Limits to her options. Yes, she could wait for another wagon train, but what then? No one was likely to have a spare team to sell, and unless she could get her hands on enough oxen or mules, the Conestoga wasn't going anywhere.

There was something else to consider. Their sons. Losing Bert was terrible enough. Rosemary refused to countenance the thought of losing their boys, as well.

Eddy was sobbing again. "I don't want you to die, Pa," he pleaded. "We love you. We need you."

Bert had to try three times before he could reply. "It's out of my hands, son. I don't want to leave you, but sometimes we don't have any say in how life treats us. I need you to be strong. I need you and your brother to look after your mother and help her out."

"What should we do, Pa?" Sam asked. "Where should we go? All the oxen are gone, and we're on our own."

"*All* the oxen?" Bert's face became paler.

All this while the mountain man had been standing a respectful distance back. Now, moving to the blanket, he remarked, "They're not completely on their own."

Bert turned his head, evidently focusing on the sound of the frontiersman's voice. "King? Is that you? Thank God!" Sliding his hand from Rosemary's, he groped the ground near King's moccasins. "Where are you?"

"Right here." Nate King squatted. His big hand enfolded Bert's, and a radiant smile lit Bert's face.

"There's hope, then! Please. I'm begging you, man to man. Do what you can to help my family make it out alive. They mean everything to me."

"I can tell," King said. "From where I sit, you've been a mighty fine father and husband."

It was a tremendously kind thing to say, and Rosemary saw how it brought tears of gratitude to Bert's eyes. His throat bobbed, and he gave King's hand a shake.

"Thank you. You don't know how glad this makes me. I can rest a little easier. I can go—" Bert stopped. His arms sagged, his fingers went limp, and he whispered in forlorn acceptance of the inevitable, "I don't have much time left. Rose, Samuel, Edward, always remember I loved you. Always remember I did what I thought best for all of us."

"Pa!" Eddy cried, and flung himself across the blanket.

Uttering a choked wail, Sam turned his head away.

Rosemary bent low and kissed Bert on the lips. His mouth curled upward in the beginnings of a return kiss he never completed. She was staring directly into his eyes and saw the spark of life fade. One instant it was there, weak but undeniable, the next instant it was as if the windows to his soul had been slammed shut and the curtains drawn. "Bertram!" she moaned, her face on his shoulder.

The three of them wept an eternity. Rosemary cried until she was totally drained, both emotionally and physically. Sniffling, she pulled Sam and Eddy to her and hugged them fiercely, then she slowly sat up. "Sam, fetch our shovels. We have a hole to dig."

"So soon?" Eddy said. "Why can't it wait until morning?"

Nate King had moved back again, leaving them to their sorrow. "The scent might bring that grizzly back," he mentioned, "or lure in another. If none of you mind, I'll do the honors while the three of you climb into the wagon and get some rest."

"At a time like this?" Sam retorted.

"You have to try," Rosemary came to the mountain man's defense. "We'll need our wits about us from here on out."

Sam rose, wiping his cheeks with the backs of his hands. "Maybe so, but I don't think it's right for a stranger to plant Pa. That's our job." He glanced at Nate King. "No insult intended."

"None taken," the mountain man said.

Rosemary struggled to her feet. She would rather do as King had suggested. She would rather curl into a ball, pull a blanket over her head, and shut out the world and everyone and everything in it. But her eldest would never forgive her if she didn't help. They had it to do, as the old saw went. "We'll bury Bert ourselves."

The digging took longer than she anticipated. The soil wasn't as soft as it seemed, not after the first four to five inches. They worked in turns. Rosemary dug until her shoulders were too sore to continue, then Sam took over. He dug and dug, enlarging the grave to twice the size she had, and would have gone longer had Ed not asked to take a hand.

Nate King stood guard a dozen yards away, his Hawken cradled in the crook of an elbow. Rosemary wouldn't have minded his help, but he didn't offer, probably as a courtesy to Sam. At one point, when Eddy was digging, King shushed them and turned toward the river.

Rosemary heard trees rustling in the wind and the distant screech of a panther. Nothing, though, to account for King's request. Then, so faint she wasn't sure if they were real or a figment of her imagination, she thought she heard the pad of stealthy footfalls. Whatever it was, it circled them, its reddish eyes blazing in the dark.

Eddy scooted to her side. Sam drew a pistol.

"No," Nate King warned. "Shoot it, and you could bring the whole pack down on our heads."

"It's a wolf?" Sam said, jerking his thumb from the hammer.

"An entire pack. The rest are nosing around the dead oxen."

Rosemary marveled anew at how sharp the mountain man's senses were. She was deaf and blind by comparison, for try as she might she couldn't hear or see any of the others. She was glad he was there. With his continued help they just might make it.

Presently, though, a new and disturbing thought intruded itself, like a worm into an apple. Here she was, placing her trust in a man she knew precious little about, in a virtual stranger, as Sam had rightly noted. King claimed to have a family of his own, but maybe he had lied. Maybe he had an ulterior motive for helping them. Not many would do as he was doing and risk their life for people they hardly knew.

What kind of person was he *really*?

Rosemary studied him on the sly. He was so large, so powerfully built, he could crush the three of them with his bare hands without half trying. She recalled the lurid tales she had been told of mountain men and their dalliances with Indian maidens. By some accounts they were as randy as goats, latter-day centaurs who delighted in ravishing the fairer sex. Was that his ulterior motive?

Rosemary's doubts and worries multiplied like rabbits. What was to stop King from having his way? They were no match for a man like him. Should the frontiersman take it into his head to dispose of them, they were as good as dead.

"You look peaked, Mrs. Spencer," the object of her anxiety said. "Maybe you should go lie down."

Rosemary's head snapped up. The mountain man had been watching her. "I'm fine, thank you," she said more testily than she intended, and promptly regretted it. There was no mistaking the genuine concern in his voice, or the sincere kindness in his eyes. She felt silly for doubting him. And yet he *was* a stranger.

Nate King turned to Sam. "I know you want to bury your father yourselves, but I'd be honored if you'd let me do some of the digging. Your mother and your brother are plumb wore out, and your hands are in no shape to go on."

Rosemary took hold of Sam's right wrist. His palm was covered with blisters. One of the largest had broken and the skin hung in loose folds. "Why didn't you tell me?"

Sam shrugged. "I'm the man of the family now. You never heard Pa complain, did you?"

No, Rosemary hadn't, in all the years of their union. He always labored without complaint, rain or shine, hot or cold, toiling in the fields from dawn until dusk and often a lot later. He had been tireless in his devotion. If ever a man deserved a fitting headstone, it was him. *Here lies Bertram Horace Spencer, loving husband, devoted father. May his soul rest in eternal peace.* Something along those lines.

Nate King had a hand on the shovel. "What do you say?"

"I guess I don't mind," Sam said. "At the rate we're going, it'll be daylight before we're finished."

King handed his Hawken to Sam and hopped into the hole. "Stand back." Dirt commenced to fly fast and furious. He dug with smooth, precise strokes, widening and deepening as he went. In a third of the time it had taken them, he had a full size grave excavated, with a small mountain of dank earth beside it. "This should do. It's deep enough so the coyotes and wolves won't dig him back up." King tossed the shovel to Sam and climbed out.

"Can I have one last look at Pa?" Eddy requested.

The mountain man had wrapped Bert in a pair of blankets and looped rope around the body. As much as Rosemary wouldn't mind a last look herself, she shook her head. By now Bert's eyes would be glazed over, and he had stiffened up. "Do you remember all those times he held you in his lap and hugged you?"

"Sure I do, Ma," Eddy said.

"Which is best? To remember him that way? Or lying in the dirt, his face all white and bloody?"

"When you put it like that," Eddy said, and bit his lower lip.

Sam needed Nate King's help lowering Bert down. Sam took the head, King the legs, and between them they eased the body onto its back.

"Ma, you say the words."

Now that the moment had arrived, Rosemary was at a loss. How did she sum up a man's life in a few short sentences? A quote from Scripture would do, but for the life of her she couldn't think of one. Her mind was as blank as an unused chalk slate. Conscious of her sons' expectant stares, she said in a rush, "We'll miss you, Bertram. You were the best husband any woman ever had, the best father any boy ever had. We'll never forget you."

Eddy began bawling.

Sam squatted and touched the mound of fresh earth. "I'm sorry I wasn't there when the bear jumped you."

"If you had been," Nate King said, "we'd be burying you, too." Then, to Rosemary's amazement, he recited the Twenty-third Psalm in its entirety. At the conclusion, he picked up a handful of dirt and scattered it over the top of the grave, intoning, "Ashes to ashes, dust to dust."

Quietly, solemnly, they returned to the Conestoga.

King said he would keep watch. Rosemary bid him goodnight and ushered her offspring into the wagon. They lay in their customary spots, Rosemary staring at empty space where Bert's chest should be. Already she missed the feel of him, the smell of him. She doubted she would be able to sleep a wink, but hardly had she closed her eyes when exhaustion sucked her into a Stygian void.

The last sound she heard was the howling of the wolves.

Chapter Seven

Rosemary snapped awake and sat up with a start. She had been in a deep, dreamless sleep, and for a few moments she stared in befuddled confusion, trying to remember where she was and what she was doing there. Images of Bert's death flooded through her, and her heart was ripped asunder. Fighting back tears, she looked up and was surprised to find the front opening in the canvas awash in golden sunlight. Usually she was up at the crack of dawn to fix breakfast for her pride and joys.

The boys! Rosemary turned, and there they were, slumbering blissfully on. Sam snored lightly. Out of habit she went to rouse them, but didn't. After the horrors of the day before, they needed all the rest they could get.

Quietly, Rosemary moved to the seat and climbed out. The sun was hours high in a serene blue sky. It was the middle of the morning. She went to lower herself over the side and received another surprise. Picketed nearby were two of their missing oxen. "How in the world?" she blurted. There was only one answer, and as she dropped lightly to the ground she caught the mouthwatering aroma of roasting meat.

The mountain man had been busy. He had constructed a lean-to and under it made a small fire. What little smoke the fire gave off was dissipated by the intertwined branches. On a small spit over the fire chunks of rabbit meat had been impaled. Beside the fire, on a flat rock, sat a coffeepot. The big bay was tethered close at hand, saddled and ready to ride.

Smoothing her dress, Rosemary went over. Nate King was seated cross-legged under the lean-to, and of all things, he was reading a book. *The Last of the Mohicans,* by James Fenimore Cooper. "Good morning," she said. The book was a handsome leather-bound edition, the pages dog-eared from use. "Reading, I see." It was a silly comment. But she quite frankly didn't know what to make of the man. He had demolished every preconceived notion she ever had of mountain men.

King straightened. "Cooper is one of my favorites," he said, inserting a folded sheet of paper to serve as a book-mark. "I have all the novels he's written so far. The Leatherstocking stories are best."

Rosemary had never read Cooper's immensely popular works, herself, but she knew the Leatherstocking series chronicled the adventures of Hawkeye, a frontiersman. "I wonder why you'd think that," she said, grinning.

"He exaggerates some, but I like his style of writing." King folded a swatch of cloth around it and slid it into a beaded leather bag. "I have about fifty books in my library now."

"*You* have a library?" Rosemary said, and wanted to sew her lips shut for being so crass.

King failed to notice. Or if he did, he was gentleman enough not to let on. "Well, I have a bookcase in the

main room of our cabin. Books are hard to come by this
far west, so whenever I need to go to St. Louis or points
east, I always buy at least one to take back with me."
Reaching into the leather bag, he produced another
folded cloth and unraveled it. "I bought this for my wife
this time around." He held it up so she could read the
title. "DOMESTIC MANNERS OF THE AMERICANS
by Frances Trollope" was emblazoned on the cover.

"Your wife?" Rosemary said. "But isn't she Sho-
shone?"

King's handsome face rippled in amusement. "She
speaks English better than I do, and reads faster, too."

Another of Rosemary's long-held beliefs was dashed
to pieces on the rocks of reality. In Missouri, Indians
were portrayed in the press and elsewhere as lacking the
mental capacity of whites. Or, as an editor once phrased
it, "Heathens are too stupid to learn to read and write.
Why, they don't even have a written language of their
own!"

The mountain man caressed the book as if it were the
woman he loved. "Winona likes to read about what
white women are doing back in the States. She can sit
and flip through a catalogue for hours."

To redeem herself, Rosemary commented, "It sounds
as if Indian women aren't much different from me."

"They're not," King said, replacing his new acquisi-
tion. "Nor are Indian men all that different from white
men."

Rosemary had to take exception. "Pardon me, but you
don't see white men going around slaughtering innocent
women and children, and lifting scalps."

King slid the parfleche to one side, then pressed a finger to a chunk of rabbit meat. "You woke up just in time.
It's almost done." He met her gaze. "Scalping was done
by whites long before the Sioux came along. In the early
days of the colonies, England put a bounty of one hun-

dred pounds on every Indian scalp whites collected. Men, women, and children." He pried a small piece of meat off and tasted it. "As for that slaughtering you talk of, have you any idea how many Indian tribes have been wiped out since Plymouth Rock?"

"No, I can't say I do," Rosemary admitted.

"Take the Creeks. In his book, Davy Crockett tells how an entire longhouse was burned to the ground with warriors, women, and children still inside. The day after the battle, some white soldiers ate potatoes they found in a root cellar underneath it." King paused. "Potatoes roasted in the body fat of the Indians who had been burnt alive. Crockett himself ate some."

At a loss to rebut his argument, Rosemary said the first thing that popped into her head. "You must think poorly of Davy Crockett."

"Not at all. He's one of the most honest souls who ever lived. He ate those potatoes because he was half-starved. I'd have done the same."

Rosemary didn't understand. She just didn't understand at all. On the one hand, the mountain man branded whites as no better than redskins. On the other, he admired someone like Davy Crockett, an admitted Indian-fighter.

Nate King removed the rabbit meat from the flames and held the stick out to her. "Care for a piece?"

"Don't mind if I do." Rosemary was famished. Yet as she slid a hot morsel onto her palm, guilt pricked her conscience. How could she eat, when hardly more than twelve hours ago she had lost her husband? She should be in mourning. By rights she shouldn't have any appetite at all.

"I figured it was best to let you and the boys sleep in," King mentioned.

"You've been busy," Rosemary said with her mouth full, a breach of etiquette she would never commit in polite society.

"I checked on the grizzly. It's long gone, but it might come back tonight for a second helping. The wolves ate most of the other two dead oxen, and they might return, too."

"What would you suggest?" Rosemary asked. "Should we go downriver and pitch camp?" Leaving the Conestoga and all their worldly goods troubled her. She couldn't afford to replace them.

"We'll stay put," King said, "and if the bear comes nosing around, we'll run him off or kill him."

"Bert tried that, remember?"

"With all due respect, ma'am, I've killed a few grizzlies in my time. Fact is, my Indian name translates as 'Grizzly Killer.'"

King's head was turned toward the wagon, and Rosemary could see the eagle feather in his hair. "You sure have taken to Indian ways."

"There's a lot we can learn from them. Indians lived here long before whites came along. They're masters at living off the land, at surviving where most of our kind couldn't. And most aren't the bloodthirsty fiends our people make them out to be."

"Tell that to the Sioux."

King bit into a piece of rabbit and chewed it before replying. "How would you feel if a foreign army invaded the United States? Would you stand by and let them do as they wanted, or would you want to rise up in arms against them?"

"That's a silly question. The War of 1812 proved Americans are willing to fight for their country and their liberty."

"Yet you blame the Indians for doing the same." King gestured at the prairie. "The Sioux have roamed this region for generations. They see it as theirs, and us as intruders. To them, we're a foreign army invading their soil. The same with the Blackfeet, the Comanches, the Utes."

David Thompson

Rosemary had never thought of the conflict in those exact terms. "So you're saying we're in the wrong and they're in the right?"

"I'm saying it's a shame our two peoples can't live together in peace," King said sadly. "The blood that's been shed so far is a drop in the bucket compared to the blood that will be shed later on. Mark my words."

Rosemary felt little sympathy for the red race after what she had witnessed the day before. To change the subject, she nodded at the recovered oxen. "Did they stray back on their own?"

"No. I tracked them down at first light. They hadn't gone far."

"What about the third one?" Rosemary asked.

"His tracks led east along the trail," King said. "I'm fixing to ride after him as soon as all of you are up and about." He squinted at the sun. "We'd better hope the Sioux don't find him first."

Rosemary swallowed more rabbit. "What difference would it make if they did?"

"The Sioux aren't stupid. None of the wagons they attacked yesterday were pulled by oxen. They're bound to wonder where he came from, and backtrack him right to your Conestoga. We don't want that."

The understatement of the year, Rosemary reflected. "Head on out, then. The boys and I will be fine." In the bright light of the new day much of her fear and anxiety had disappeared. Then she glanced at the mound of dirt, and her loss hit her with the impact of a sledgehammer.

Nate King was rising with his bag and the Hawken. "If you're sure," he said. "I shouldn't be gone more than an hour, at most." He wasted no time forking leather. "No loud noises. And don't let your younguns stray off." Smiling, he tapped his heels against the bay.

Rosemary watched him leave with trepidation. He was all that stood between her family and three more unmarked graves. She poured herself some coffee and sat sipping it until the Conestoga creaked and a tousled head of hair was framed in the opening.

"Morning, Ma." Samuel yawned and stretched, shook himself like a dog will when it's wet, and dropped to the ground. "Was that Mr. King I heard riding off?"

"He'll be back soon," Rosemary said, and filled her oldest in on the current state of affairs. Sam helped himself to a slightly singed morsel of rabbit and sank his teeth into it with relish.

"That Mr. King sure is something. I don't mind confessing I was a little scared of him at first. He's so huge and all. And when he looks at me, it's as if he's looking right through me." Sam chomped with his mouth open. "If that makes any sense."

Rosemary had experienced the same unnerving sensation. "We should thank the Lord he came along when he did. If we're real nice, maybe we can persuade him to stay with us until the next wagon train shows up."

"If one does," Sam mentioned.

As if there weren't enough uncertainties in Rosemary's life, she also had to face the possibility that another train would not come. Supposedly, another was due to set out, but that was hearsay, information a clerk imparted to Bert. What if the clerk had been mistaken? She and her sons couldn't wait indefinitely.

"Ma?" Out of the wagon poked her youngest, his normally bright and cheery features downcast. "Is it true? Or did I have a bad dream?"

Rosemary rose. Eddy's gaze drifted past her and a pitiable groan escaped him. He was out of the wagon and in her arms before she had gone four steps. Crying bitterly, he buried his face in her dress. At a loss to know what to say to soothe his hurt and ebb his tears, Rosemary placed her hands on his slim shoulders and stood stock-still while he cried himself out.

A lump formed in Rosemary's throat, but her own eyes remained dry. She wondered why that should be. Was there something wrong with her? The love of her life had died and she wasn't half as devastated as her son. She told herself it was because she couldn't afford to break down. Not now, with their lives in imminent peril. She had to keep a level head for their sakes, if not her own.

Sam saved plenty of meat for them. When Eddy's sobs dwindled to sniffles, Rosemary ushered him under the lean-to. He accepted a chunk but ate with wooden disinterest.

Rosemary was bending to pour herself a second cup of King's delicious coffee when a shadow flitted across them. Instinctively dropping low, she craned her neck and beheld the cause. A large buzzard was soaring in a circle high overhead, and he wasn't alone. Five of his feathered cousins were performing aerial pirouettes with deceptive grace. And to the west were twenty to thirty more, converging above the site of the massacre.

One banked suddenly and plummeted sharply earthward. Cottonwoods blocked Rosemary's view of the last stage of its descent, but she knew where it had alighted. "I'll be right back," she said, and hastened into the wagon for her rifle and pistol.

If the buzzards heard her approach, they gave no sign. A dozen were feasting on the pair of dead oxen, their big beaks rending and ripping with grisly abandon.

Rosemary imagined even more were scavenging the dead members of the wagon train, but she had no hankering to go see. About to retrace her steps, she idly scanned the Platte in both directions. Far to the west something moved, something large. She screened her eyes with a palm, but whatever it was had vanished into the woods.

Sam and Eddy were talking in hushed voices, so engrossed in their discussion they didn't hear her until she was right on top of them. Both jumped when she stepped into the lean-to, and Eddy rose to flee.

"It's only me," Rosemary said, and chuckled. "But if I

were a Sioux, you two would be bald before your time."

Neither grinned at her jest. Eddy nudged Sam, who shook his head, so Eddy cleared his throat and fidgeted as he did whenever she caught him with his hand in the cookie jar. "Ma, we've got an idea. It's Sam's brainstorm, but I think we should go along."

Rosemary looked from one to the other. "Go along with what?"

"Hear us out before you say anything," Sam interposed. "We need it more than they do, and it would be a shame to let it go to waste."

"Need what?" Rosemary said, mystified.

"Money," Eddy said.

"Now, where would we get our hands on—" Rosemary started to ask, and the answer leaped out at her like a rabid wolf. Shocked beyond measure, she declared, "You can't be thinking what I think you're thinking!"

"Mr. Kastner had a poke filled with bills and coins," Sam said. "I saw it with my own eyes. Some of the other men carried their money on them, too, not in their wagons. The savages have no use for it, so the money must still be in their pockets."

"You want to steal from the dead?" Rosemary couldn't have been more outraged if they had committed cold-blooded murder. "You want to strip those poor people of the last shred of dignity they have left?"

"What dignity?" Sam challenged. "They're *dead*. They're past caring what we do. So why not help ourselves before the animals rip their clothes apart to get at their bodies?"

"Samuel Spencer, you hush!" Rosemary said sternly. Wheeling, she tramped to the Conestoga and stood in its shadow, her thoughts in a whirl. The very notion was barbaric! And yet they *could* use more money. A new house, a new barn, wouldn't come cheap. Hundreds of dollars was theirs for the taking if they had the grit—and strong enough stomachs.

Rosemary couldn't believe she was seriously considering the proposition. But it wouldn't take long. Two minutes there, ten minutes to go through pockets and purses, another two minutes to make it back. What harm would there be other than to her innate sense of decency?

Sam and Eddy were persistent when they wanted to be. "Have you thought it over?" her oldest inquired, joining her. "Because if we're going to do it, we should get it over with before they become too ripe."

"What an awful thing to say," Rosemary scolded, and yet, he had a valid point. "Very well. Grab your guns. Sam, you empty out the pouch with our lye soap and bring it along to tote the money back. There's no telling how much there will be, and how much will be in coin."

Both boys lit up like candles. They scurried to obey while Rosemary walked to the rear of the wagon and peered eastward. They had a good half an hour yet before Nate King returned, plenty of time to accomplish their abhorrent task. She preferred he not find out. He was bound to think less of her.

Word had spread among the vulture community. More than thirty were feeding, and more were circling aloft. They were reluctant to leave their food and hissed in anger when Sam and Eddy rushed from the underbrush, shouting and waving their arms to drive the carrion eaters off. Only when Sam swung his rifle like a club and clipped one did the buzzards leap up, their wings flapping furiously to become airborne. Soon a black cloud circled above them, waiting for Rosemary and her sons to leave so they could resume their interrupted meals.

Rosemary turned to the corpses, and her resolve melted like butter under a hot sun. The bodies were in much worse condition. Eyes, noses, ears, and the soft, fleshy parts of the face and neck had been ripped out and devoured. Clothes had been partially torn off, and the vultures had gotten at the bellies and thighs. Coils of intestines lay fermenting in the heat like so many over-cooked sausages.

The spectacle was horrible enough; the increasing stench only made it worse. Rosemary covered her mouth with a hand and breathed shallow, but she still smelled the revolting reek. "Maybe we should forget about this," she said.

"Stay back if you want. Me and Eddy will search them," Sam proposed.

"Eddy and I," Rosemary corrected, but he wasn't listening. Sam had bent over Percy Ostman and was going through the old man's pockets.

Eddy was next to Charley Kastner, or what was left of the braggart, riveted to the ravaged travesty that had once been Kastner's moon face.

Rosemary beckoned to him. "Edward, if you're not up to this, leave it to your brother." She didn't blame him for being squeamish. She felt downright ill.

"I can do it, Ma." Scrunching up his nerve, Eddy hunkered and ran his hands over Kastner's tattered clothes. Patting a pocket, he exclaimed, "I found something!" He hurried to her carrying a bloodstained leather poke. His fingers were covered with gore, and when he handed it to her, some smeared onto her fingers.

Grimacing, Rosemary leaned her rifle against her leg, loosened the tie string, and upended the poke over her palm. Out spilled so many coins that several fell to the ground. Last to slide out was a wad of bills thick enough to gag a dog.

"There must be a hundred dollars," Eddy declared.

"A lot more than that," Rosemary said, and squatted to count it. The Kastners weren't wealthy, so the contents of the poke must be the sum total of their life's savings, a whopping four hundred and eighty-eight dollars.

Sam came running over, all excited. "Look at what I found!"

David Thompson

Gold pieces, fourteen of them, several spattered with drops of dried blood. Rosemary added them to the pile. "Keep looking." Her squeamishness gone, she helped search, going from body to body until they had checked every adult. Seven rings, a silver necklace, and a fob watch were also collected.

"Land sakes," Eddy said in awe. "We're rich."

"Not hardly." Rosemary counted the money twice to be sure. The grand total came to one thousand, seven hundred, and fifty-five dollars. Combined with the money they had left from the sale of their farm, they had enough to last them years. And that didn't include the value of the rings or other jewelry.

Sam was gazing thoughtfully westward. "There's more for the taking, you know, just a short ways down the trail."

Rosemary knew he was alluding to the settlers in the last three wagons, and Harry Trapp. The pilot had carried a substantial poke of his own. Since his fee was two hundred dollars per wagon, he must have close to two thousand on him. A tempting sum, to put it mildly.

"What about the Indians?" Eddy asked.

What about them? Rosemary reflected. Nate King had said they might return, but here it was almost noon and none had showed up. It could be they weren't coming back. So why not go see?

"The schooners can't have gotten that far, Ma," Sam said, "not with the Sioux after them. We can be there and back before you know it. And if Mr. King asks where we've been, we'll tell him we were scouting around for Indian sign."

"You think of everything, don't you?" Rosemary said, her sarcasm tempered by her appreciation. She debated the dangers, weighed them against the value of another two thousand dollars—or more—to her family, and slung the pouch over her shoulder. "Walk quickly and stay close together."

96

Sam took the lead, his rifle tucked to his shoulder. The rutted track meandered according to the flow of the Platte. Hoofprints of Sioux war horses overlay the tracks of the wagons they had chased.

Discarded items littered the trail. In a futile bid to lighten their loads and outdistance the war party, the panic struck emigrants had chucked everything— clothes, utensils, tools, food, and more.

Along a straight stretch hemmed by trees on one side and tall grass on the other, the Sioux had struck. Here lay Mr. Ferguson, mutilated almost beyond recognition. Buzzards flew off at Sam's rush, and within moments he had found Ferguson's wallet. "Another two hundred and forty dollars!"

Slain in the act of fleeing, irregularly spaced bodies were sprawled on either side of the three charred wagons. Rosemary avoided looking at the children. A ruby ring on Mrs. Crane's finger proved difficult to remove, the finger was so swollen. Rosemary solved the problem by spitting on it and working the ring back and forth.

Sam and Eddy scurried about like chipmunks, eagerly gathering valuables. Rosemary's pouch was soon bulging. As yet, there was no sign of the pilot. She scoured the woods along the river and the grassland, and was about convinced Harry Trapp had gotten away when Eddy hollered.

The pilot had been stripped naked, thrown onto his back on top of a large log, and tied down, hands and feet. Then the Sioux had whittled on him as if he were a block of wood. Why they had tortured him and no one else mystified Rosemary. Maybe he had aroused their wrath by fighting back. Or maybe the Sioux knew he was the leader of the train, and the torture was their way of paying him back for bringing whites into their territory.

Trapp's clothes had been left where they were thrown. Sam scooped up Trapp's jacket, and Eddy found Trapp's pants. But it was in the pilot's right boot that Rosemary stumbled on what they were looking for: one thousand, eight hundred, and eighty-five dollars in various denominations.

"Are we rich *now*?" Eddy asked.

"No, but we're close," Rosemary said, grinning from ear to ear. In a day and age when most laborers earned three to four hundred dollars a year, they now had a small fortune. Close to four thousand dollars in cash and coins alone.

"We had the right idea, then, didn't we?" Sam crowed.

"Yes, you did," Rosemary admitted. Now all they had to do was reach Oregon alive.

As if on cue, from out of the high grass came a whinny and the thud of hooves. Horses were approaching.

The Sioux had returned, after all.

Chapter Eight

Rosemary Spencer grabbed her youngest by the collar and raced into waist-high weeds. Sam was only a step behind them. Squatting, she gazed across the Oregon Trail just as the buffalo grass parted and out of it emerged four riders.

They weren't Sioux. They were an assorted bunch, these newcomers. Two were white, big men like Nate King. But where his buckskins were clean and in good condition, their buckskins were grimy and shabby. Where his beard was neatly clipped, their beards were dirty, unkempt tangles. And where the mountain man had pride in keeping his face and hands clean, these two hadn't washed in a month of Sundays. They looked enough alike to be twins, except one had black hair and the other brown. Both were armed with Hawkens, a brace of pistols, and long knives.

The third rider was short and thin, a ferret in filthy buckskins who favored a raccoon hat complete with a long tail. He wasn't white, but he wasn't an Indian, either. Rosemary pegged him as a half-breed and recollected hearing that 'breeds, as they were called, were a vicious lot by nature. Whether true or not, the thin rider had a frightening aspect about him. A jagged scar on the left side of his face had a lot to do with it. The scar ran from his jaw to the corner of his left eye and must have been a fearsome wound. When it healed, the skin had mended unevenly, lending his face a twisted, inhuman appearance.

The last rider was definitely an Indian, although Rosemary couldn't say from which tribe. Like his companions he wore buckskins, only his were beaded and cleaner than theirs. He also wore knee-high moccasins. A bow was in his left hand, and a quiver crammed full of feathered shafts lay across his back. He rode bareback.

The quartet rode into the open and surveyed the burned wagons and the bodies.

"I told you, didn't I?" the half-breed remarked. "When the wind is right I can smell rotting flesh a mile away."

"That nose of yours never ceases to amaze me, Chaco," said the black-haired giant. "Even Kicking Bull, here, can't match you."

The Indian made a sniffing noise as if he were insulted, but he didn't say a word.

"No one can match me, Gault," Chaco said. "Kicking Bull hasn't been living in the wild as long as I have. He's too used to village life. His senses are dull." The half-breed smirked. "So are yours and your brother's."

"How you can fit such an oversized head on those scrawny shoulders of yours is beyond me," Gault countered. "You're about the most in-love-with-himself jasper Garvey and me ever met."

"Every coon should know his limitations," Chaco said.

The other giant, Garvey, chuckled. "Yeah, but to hear you talk, you ain't got any. Sometimes you act as if you're damned near perfect."

100

"I am," Chaco said, and they all laughed, even the Indian. Chaco dismounted and dropped to one knee beside a bloated body. "Now to business. These pilgrims are ripe for plucking."

The others climbed down and moved from victim to victim. It didn't take them long to realize something was amiss. Gault rose and scratched his black beard. "I don't get it. None of the pilgrims I've checked have money or jewelry on them."

"The same here," Garvey said.

Chaco finished examining Mrs. Crane. "This woman was wearing a ring. See the mark on her index finger? But the ring's not here now."

"The Sioux, you reckon?" Gault said.

"Since when do they take cash and coins?" Chaco rejoined. "All they're interested in are scalps and a few trinkets for their squaws." The 'breed slowly rose. "If I didn't know better, boys, I'd swear someone beat us to it."

"Maybe someone did," Garvey growled, and menacingly hefted his rifle. "They'll regret it if we get our hands on them. This was our idea. We've been doing it for months now, and meddlers aren't allowed."

Rosemary couldn't believe what she was hearing. These four were scavengers of a two-legged variety, human buzzards who made their living, if it could be called that, by stealing from the dead.

"Kicking Bull, find out which way they went," Chaco directed.

Eddy's fingers dug into Rosemary's wrist. She had to get them out of there, but they were too close to the Oregon Trail. Any movement, however slight, was bound to be detected. She caught Sam's eye and he bobbed his head, suggesting they back away.

Rosemary balked until she saw the Indian bent low at the very spot she had been kneeling when she removed Mrs. Crane's ring. Taking Eddy's free hand, she quietly stepped backward. The weeds rustled and she froze, dreading an outcry. But Kicking Bull was still examining the ground, and the other three were busy talking. She took another step, placing her foot down lightly so as not to make any noise. Eddy imitated her. Sam came last, covering them.

Kicking Bull unfurled and called out to Chaco, who went over to see what the warrior had found.

Rosemary moved faster. She had to. At any moment the foursome would follow their tracks into the vegetation. She angled toward the Platte. Along the river the undergrowth wasn't as dense and they could travel swiftly. Another couple of strides, and they were out of sight of the trail and in among cottonwoods. Pivoting, she ran, nearly pulling Eddy off his feet in her haste.

Sam matched their pace, sidestepping so he could spot pursuit instantly.

The trees ended at a grassy bank at the river's edge. Rosemary moved to the lip and looked down. Close in to shore the Platte was only six inches deep, if that. "They can't track us in water," she whispered. Bracing her left hand on the bank, she lowered herself down, careful not to splash. "Now you two."

Eddy needed help, but Sam slid lithely over and waited for them to head downstream ahead of him.

Crouched low, Rosemary hugged the shoreline. She smiled inwardly at her clever ruse, confident they would give the four cutthroats the slip. Her shoes sank a bit with each step, and she noticed that the river bottom was muddy. Every time she lifted a foot, a small cloud mushroomed outward. Hoping the cutthroats wouldn't spot the muddy water, she hurried eastward.

Too late, Rosemary heard Sam's whispered warning and spied a pair of mallard ducks just ahead. At sight of them the ducks quacked in alarm and took wing, raising a considerable racket.

"Quick!" Rosemary urged. Making more noise than

she liked, they waded around the next bend and ducked down.

"Did you hear those ducks?" a gruff voice hollered.

"Garvey, go have a look-see," Chaco directed.

Rosemary eased high enough to see over the bank. Figures were moving about in the trees. One slanted toward the river. A second later Garvey's sizable bulk strode into sight. He saw the ducks winging toward the opposite side of the Platte, and he turned right and left, seeking whatever it was that spooked them.

Rosemary had a clear shot. The range wasn't more than thirty yards, but killing him would constitute cold-blooded murder. Claiming self-defense wouldn't wash. He hadn't harmed her, or hers. She suspected he might, given half the chance, but that didn't justify taking so drastic a step.

Then Rosemary sensed movement beside her, and out of the corner of her eye she saw her oldest sighting down the barrel of his long rifle. Putting a restraining hand on his forearm, she shook her head.

Sam frowned, the look of disapproval he gave her sufficient to show he thought she was making a mistake. But his thumb relaxed on the hammer and he raised his chin from the smooth walnut stock.

Garvey had moved to near where they'd entered the water and was gazing in their general direction.

Rosemary was pierced by terror. She stood rooted in place, thinking he must have spotted them, but after gazing across the Platte he turned and shambled into the cottonwoods.

"That overstuffed jackass couldn't see a cow if it was right in front of him," Sam whispered.

Ordinarily, Rosemary would tell him to mind his language, but under the circumstances she chose fit to overlook his lapse. Firming her hold on Eddy, she pivoted and continued downriver. They had a long way to go before they would reach the Conestoga, and she desperately yearned to get there. Nate King must be back by now, and he would know how to deal with the four thieves.

Her hypocrisy was like a slap in the face. How dare she brand them as thieves when she and her sons were guilty of the same sin!

Maybe they posed no threat whatsoever, although her intuition hinted otherwise. And long ago she had learned, often the hard way, that her intuition was more often reliable than not.

Fifty yards they traveled. A hundred. Rosemary began to relax, believing they had given the quartet the slip. She rounded a bend and was considering stepping out onto dry land, when Eddy suddenly squeezed her fingers and yanked on her arm so hard, she winced.

"A snake, Ma!"

Rosemary saw a sinuous brown form gliding off into the river. A harmless water snake, but the harm had been done. Eddy's cry might have been loud enough for Chaco's bunch to hear.

"Dang you, Eddy!" Sam whispered.

"It's not his fault," Rosemary said, slogging swiftly forward. And it really wasn't. Her youngest had been deathly afraid of snakes since he was old enough to toddle. One day while she was off shopping in Holstein, Bert had found a garter snake and shown it to the boys. When Ed handled it too roughly, the snake bit him. He'd bawled and bawled even though the bite hadn't broken his skin, and ever since, the sight of a serpent was enough to induce a panic.

Sam kept glancing over his shoulder. "No sign of those polecats yet," he reported.

"Let's hope they didn't hear." Rosemary slanted onto a gravel bar that jutted into the river like an accusing finger. Their feet dripping wet, they were soon huddled in a stand of timber. "How are you holding up?" she asked her youngest.

"Just fine, Ma." Eddy avoided meeting her gaze. "Sorry about yelling like that. I didn't mean to."

"What's done is done," Rosemary quoted her grandmother's favorite saying, and hugged him. "Now let's light a shuck before I see a mouse and do the same thing." Her fear of mice was a long-standing family joke.

Eddy grinned and whispered, "Thanks, Ma."

It was forty-five minutes before they reached the Conestoga. Rosemary repeatedly stopped to listen and scan behind them. Once she thought she heard hoofbeats on the Oregon Trail, but she couldn't be sure. Her joy on reaching the wagon was unbounded. They were safe! She leaned against it, giving silent thanks for their deliverance, but her elation was short-lived.

"Where's Mr. King?" Sam asked. "Shouldn't he have been back by now?"

Rosemary straightened, her intuition blaring again. Something was wrong, dreadfully wrong. Nate King struck her as a man of his word. When he said he wouldn't be gone more than an hour, she could take it as gospel. He was long overdue, and the only possible explanation was that he had run into trouble. She shuddered to think how they would survive without him. He had to return. He just *had* to.

Sam and Eddy materialized beside her. "We're mighty hungry. Do you mind if we rekindle the fire and warm up the rest of the meat?"

"The scent of smoke carries a long way," Rosemary reminded them. "It's best if you hold off a while."

"But the wind is blowing from the northwest to the southeast," Sam observed.

The tops of the trees confirmed his statement. They were, indeed, bending slightly to the southeast with each gust. So the smell of smoke would be carried away from Chaco and his friends, not toward them. Still, Rosemary didn't like the element of risk involved. "Hold off another half an hour, to be safe."

"How about some jerky, then?" Sam asked.

"Help yourselves."

The boys climbed into the Conestoga, and cradling her rifle, Rosemary walked toward the Oregon Trail. Once there she would have a clear view to the east and might spot Nate King. The woods around her were uncommonly still, which she attributed to her presence. A weeping willow towered before her, its leaves shimmering, and she passed under it into dappled shadow. It was so quiet, so peaceful, that Rosemary leaned her rifle against the trunk and sat down. What with losing Bert, and losing sleep, and their morning trek, she felt tired and drained. A nap would perk her up, but she wasn't about to sleep. Leaning back, she closed her eyes. She would rest a minute. Only a minute. Or maybe two. Then she would get up and go look for Nate King.

Only a minute . . .

Rosemary's eyes opened. Something had awakened her. She was uncertain what, exactly, but she was glad it had, because judging by the shadows she had slept the better part of an hour. She placed her hands flat to push to her feet, then paused.

A horse had nickered.

Nate King, Rosemary supposed, and rose and turned toward the trail. A riderless horse was contentedly grazing grass not ten yards away, its reins dangling. A dun, not King's big bay, a dun Rosemary had seen earlier. It was Gault's horse, and if it was there, its owner must be somewhere nearby. She reached for her rifle.

"Looking for this, ma'am?"

Rosemary spun, and stared into the muzzle of her own rifle, trained on her by the smirking giant.

Gault's dark eyes bore a sinister gleam. "I had to pinch myself when I saw you. I couldn't believe you were real. How is it the Sioux didn't slit your pretty throat?"

Too flabbergasted to reply, Rosemary dipped her hand toward the pistol at her waist.

"I wouldn't, were I you," Gault advised, and relieved her of the flintlock. "Why did you want to go and do that? Have I tried to hurt you? Hell, no. I've been watching you sleep for minutes and didn't harm a hair on your pretty head."

"What do you want?" Rosemary found her voice.

"Don't you want to introduce yourself first?" Gault clucked like an irate rooster. "If you ask me, you've got atrocious manners, lady. You're acting as if I'm your enemy."

Rosemary couldn't resist. "Aren't you?" she bluntly demanded.

"Whatever gave you that idea?" Gault lowered her rifle and stepped back. His own was propped against the willow. "Me and those I'm with are as friendly as can be. We'll prove it to you tonight."

The thinly veiled threat confirmed Rosemary's worst fears. "There are others with you?" She stalled, shifting so she could see the Conestoga. That close, it was plainly visible, despite the camouflage. Her sons were nowhere to be seen. Had they been harmed? Or were they resting?

"There's four of us," Gault said. "We left St. Louis three months ago bound for the Rocky Mountains."

"And you're taking your sweet time getting there," Rosemary remarked.

Gault's bushy right eyebrow formed a tepee. "What is it with you, gal? You're as contrary as a cougar with a thorn in its paw." He motioned at the Conestoga, then snagged his Hawken. "Gather whatever you want to take along and we'll go show you off to my brother and the rest."

"I don't want to," Rosemary said. She would die before she let him get any nearer to her boys.

"It's not as if you have a say in the matter. We're going for a ride, and that's that. It's no skin off my hide if you don't want to take anything along." Gault swiveled toward the dun. "Move those long legs of yours. My brother and me will come back later for a look in your wagon."

Praying her sons wouldn't spot her and call out, Rosemary walked toward the Oregon Trail. She racked her brain for a means to disarm Gault, but he was twice her size, and from the looks of him, as strong as a bull.

"What's in that pouch you're toting?" Gault unexpectedly asked. "The way you keep holding your hand over it, it must be important."

Chiding herself for being so careless, Rosemary lowered her arm and shrugged. "A few womanly things, is all."

"That war paint you gals dab on your faces? Perfume, maybe? Hand it over. I'd like to see."

"Later, why don't you," Rosemary hedged. There was no predicting how he'd react if he found the money. "We should leave while we can. I saw some Sioux in the area earlier."

"The Sioux haven't been here since yesterday," Gault said. "Stop right there and give me that damn pouch, or else." To stress his point, he touched the Hawken's barrel to her shoulder blade. "Don't think because you're a lady I won't slap you around if you give me cause."

"I don't doubt that one bit." Rosemary's bitterness was transparent.

"You sure have a mouth on you. But what woman doesn't?" Gault jabbed her with so much force, it spun her partway around. Casting her rifle aside, he grabbed the strap to the pouch and roughly hiked it over her head and down her arm. "Don't look at me like that. I asked you real nice." He stepped back and shook the pouch, and it jingled noisily. "I'll be." He shook it again, harder, and grinned. "I have me a notion what's in here. And if I'm right, you're not the lady I took you for." He dropped onto one knee, covering her with the Hawken.

Rosemary was helpless. She watched him upend the pouch, watched his eyes widen like saucers and his mouth split in astonishment, revealing teeth as yellow as corn.

"I'll be a son of a bitch! Look at all this! You've gone and done our work for us!" Gault laughed uproariously and slapped his thigh. "Wait until the others get a gander at your collection. You're a girl after our own hearts. Maybe Chaco will let you throw in with us if you please him."

Rosemary was on the verge of stating she would do no such thing when the fruit of her womb appeared behind her captor. Two rifle hammers were thumbed back simultaneously, and at the metallic clicks, Gault turned to marble.

"Be mighty careful, mister," Sam warned in his most adult tone. "If you so much as twitch wrong, my brother and I will blow out your wick."

"Hold on there," Gault rumbled. Thrusting his arms out from his sides, he let the Hawken fall. "I wasn't fixing to hurt her. Honest!"

Sam and Eddy sidled to the right, giving the scalawag a wide berth. "Want me to part his hair with lead, Ma?"

Gault looked as if he were about to lay an egg. "Kids!" he exclaimed. "Nothing but a measly pair of runts! And I fell for it." He started to rise.

"Don't even think it," Sam growled. "We might be kids, but we know how to shoot. And this close we couldn't miss if we tried."

Rosemary had to hand it to Samuel. His face was flinthard and his rifle was rock-steady. In the past twentyfour hours he had done a lot of growing up. They all had.

A crafty expression came over Gault. "I ain't about to be bucked out in gore by two sprouts who aren't old enough to shave. It would be embarrassing. My brother would never let me hear the end of it."

"Toss your artillery," Sam ordered. "Pretend you're a turtle. My trigger finger is itching up a storm."

Molasses flowed faster than Gault moved as he willingly obliged. "I'll remember this, boy," he said good-naturedly, yet with an undercurrent of menace. "We'll see how you like it when it's my turn to crow."

Eddy was scared but bravely masking his fear. "We were napping, Ma. It's a good thing Sam heard this lunkhead bellowing like a moose."

"Lunkhead, am I?" Gault said, glowering. "I'll remember you, too, you little weasel. Don't think I won't."

"Spare us your threats," Rosemary directed. Exercising care not to step between her sons and Gault, she gathered up the man's weapons and her own rifle. She also replaced the money in her pouch and slung the strap across her chest. "Let's take this no-account to the wagon. We'll tie him to a wheel until we make up our minds what to do with him."

As docile as a lamb, Gault went along. He sat with his back to the spokes and chortled when Rosemary applied rope to his wrists. "Tie them good and tight, ma'am. You don't want me to slip loose in the middle of the night and strangle the three of you in your sleep."

Eddy's mask crumbled. "Would he do that, Ma? Really and truly?"

"You bet I would," Gault answered. "I've planted kids younger than you. Most were Injuns. But it doesn't make any never mind to me if you're red or white. You're holding a gun on me. You deserve to be fed to the worms."

Rosemary's resentment knew no bounds. Before she quite realized what she was doing, she had balled her fist and smashed Gault across the mouth. The blow rocked his head back and brought a drop of blood to his upper lip, but he tossed it off with another laugh.

"Not bad, lady. A rock would do better, but I don't reckon you have it in you to beat a man senseless when he can't defend himself."

"Try me and find out," Rosemary blustered. She had never killed or maimed anyone in her life. It had always been her belief that people could get along without resorting to violence. Bert always disputed her, saying the world was violent by nature and it was silly to think that just because she was kind and decent at heart, everyone else must be. "The world was the way it is long before we were born," she remembered him asserting, "and it will go on being the way it is long after we're gone. You can ignore the ugliness, you can stick your head in the sand like one of those ostriches we've read about, but that won't make the violence go away." Rosemary regretted that Bert wasn't there now so she could admit to his face he had been right all along.

Gault tested the ropes, his smile widening. "I take it you've had a lot of practice trussing folks up, gorgeous?"

"Mister, you talk too much," Sam said, taking a step and centering his rifle on the other's brow.

Not the least bit intimidated, Gault responded, "You like to squeeze the trigger, don't you, boy? I reckon you've killed your share of deer and squirrels back home, is that it? Well, killing a man ain't the same. It takes more courage than most have."

"I can do it if I have to."

Gault's eyes bored into her oldest, and he slowly nodded. "I'll be damned. Yes, you could, couldn't you? Fair enough. I won't take you lightly from here on out. Do me the same courtesy."

Putting her hands on her hips, Rosemary backed off. "Enough talk about killing. I didn't raise my son to turn out like you."

"I doubt he'll live that long," Gault said, and snickered.

Eddy had lowered his rifle's stock to the ground and was leaning on the barrel. "You sure are in a good mood, mister."

"That's because I know something you don't, boy."

"What might that be?" Eddy asked.

Gault's next smirk was positively masterful. "I know my three pards are right behind you."

Chapter Nine

Rosemary Spencer clutched her pistol and whirled. She envisioned the other three cutthroats with their rifles leveled, envisioned herself and her sons being shot to pieces like so many wild dogs. Acute horror seized her, more for her boys than for herself. They were so young. They had their whole lives ahead of them. She swept her pistol up and out, thumbing back the hammer as she leveled it. She had never unlimbered a pistol so swiftly in her life, but it was all for nothing.

No one was there.

Stupefied, Rosemary glanced wildly about. Empty forest mocked her. She looked at Sam, who was as confused as she was, and at Eddy, whose pallor was akin to a sheet's, then heard Gault's merry roar of mirth.

"You should see your faces! Three idiots, falling for the oldest trick there is!" His glee was sadistic.

Suddenly Sam sprang, gouging the muzzle of his rifle

against the man's forehead. "Enough! I know what you're trying to do."

Gault's laughter died. "Figured it out, did you, boy?"

"Figured what out?" Rosemary said, at a loss.

"His friends can't be that far off, Ma," Sam said. "He's hoping they'll hear us and come to his rescue."

Rosemary should have thought of that herself. She was the parent. But she wasn't devious by nature, she never had been, which made her easy prey for those who were. "Not another sound out of you, Gault."

"Or what? Your son will shoot me? My pards are bound to hear. So go ahead. I dare you."

Sam lowered his rifle, palmed his hunting knife, and jabbed the razor-sharp tip into Gault's neck deep enough to draw blood. "Who said anything about using a gun?"

Gault turned as red as a beet. "Gloat while you can. You're not as smart as you think. None of you are."

Rosemary wondered what he was alluding to. Suddenly, like a bolt out of the blue, insight dawned, and she turned toward the Oregon Trail. "His horse! He left it out in the open, where the others are bound to find it."

"Let's go," Sam said, already in motion.

"No." Rosemary hurried past him. "I'll tend to his animal myself. Stand guard here until I get back." She smiled at Eddy, who clearly wasn't pleased that she was leaving. "It won't take long. Help your brother keep an eye on this ruffian."

"Do I shoot him if he tries to hurt us, Ma?"

"You have my permission to shoot him dead," Rosemary said, and was treated to a few choice curses from Gault.

Sparrows were frolicking in bushes near the trail, which Rosemary construed as a sign that none of the other cutthroats were anywhere near. The dun was peacefully dozing in the hot sun, and didn't shy when

113

David Thompson

she reached for its reins. "That's a good horse," she said soothingly. "Come along nice and quietly." She led the animal into the trees.

No sooner had she done so than the dun pricked its ears and turned its head to the west.

Three riders had just rounded the bend.

Praying she hadn't been spotted, Rosemary drew the dun deeper. Chaco, Garvey, and Kicking Bull were riding three abreast, rifles across their saddles. The former and the latter had their attention fixed on the ground. Garvey was scouring the adjacent plain.

Halting in the shadow of an oak, Rosemary placed a hand over the dun's muzzle. "Hush now," she whispered.

The three human predators came to where the dun had been and rode on by.

Rosemary grinned. "They're not very good trackers, are they?" she whispered, and had the question figuratively crammed back down her throat when Kicking Bull swung his pinto around.

"What is it?" Garvey asked.

"Your brother stop here," the Indian said in clipped English, pointing at the exact spot. "He walk off. His horse go there."

Rosemary's skin crawled as the Indian's arm rose and his finger pointed directly at her hiding place. She didn't have a moment to lose. They were bound to spot her within seconds. Worse, they might spot the Conestoga, and she couldn't let that happen. She had to lure them away from her sons. To that end, she grabbed hold of the saddle and swung up. Her dress bunched around the middle of her thighs, but it couldn't be helped. Smacking her rifle against the dun's flank, she lit out of there as if she were fleeing a forest fire. She galloped eastward, away from the Conestoga, away from Sam and Eddy.

Shouts erupted. When Rosemary looked back all three were after her. During her childhood she had ridden a lot, but not much since, and her horsemanship was rusty.

114

Concentrating, she rode like a madwoman, heedless of the threat to life and limb. She ducked low branches, dodged others. She goaded the dun over logs and small boulders. She rode as she had never ridden before, but it wasn't enough.

Chaco and his companions were gaining.

The woods were to blame. Closely spaced trunks and heavy thickets were slowing Rosemary down. She needed open ground. With lusty whoops ringing in her ears, she reined toward the Oregon Trail. The cutthroats laughed and shouted back and forth. To them the chase was some kind of game. But not to her. Too much was at stake.

Ahead the trees thinned. Without slowing, Rosemary came to the trail and reined sharply to the right. The dun was racing flat out, yet her next glance showed that the Indian would soon overtake her. His pinto was fleeter than mercury. Rosemary smacked the dun's flanks a few more times, but it was wasted effort.

A bend rushed toward them. Rosemary twisted and attempted to aim her rifle with one hand. It was much too heavy.

Kicking Bull was grinning. He had slung his bow over his shoulder to free both arms, and now, in a burst of speed, he brought the pinto alongside the dun, leaned in, and wrapped a bronzed arm around her waist.

Rosemary swatted at him, but the rifle stock glanced off his chest, and a heartbeat later she was yanked from the saddle and sent tumbling. Unprepared for the fall, she hit hard on her shoulder and rolled. She wound up on her back with the breath knocked out of her. The rifle had gone sailing from her fingers, but she still had her pistol, and struggling onto her elbows, she groped for it. Her hand was swatted aside.

"Be still." Kicking Bull stood over her and pushed her flat with the sole of his moccasin. His right hand strayed to the bone hilt of his knife.

David Thompson

A cloud of dust heralded Chaco and Garvey, who leaped from their mounts while the horses were still in motion. Rushing up on either side, they looked down at her in amazement.

"Who the hell are you, woman?" Chaco demanded. "And where the hell did you come from?"

"More to the point," Garvey said, "what the hell is she doing on my brother's horse?"

Rosemary glared defiantly. She didn't dare tell them where Gault was.

"Are you deaf, woman?" Chaco said, and kicked her.

Pain exploded up Rosemary's side. She would have doubled over, except Kicking Bull had his foot on her pouch, effectively pinning her.

Bending down, Garvey entwined his thick fingers into her hair. "Where's my brother, damn it?" He shook her, none too gently. "Answer me, or by God I'll make you wish you had."

"She must be from the wagon train," Chaco speculated. "Somehow she escaped the Sioux and has been hiding."

"Which still doesn't explain where Gault is." Garvey was a brutish man; anger made him uglier. "Last chance, bitch. Tell me what I want to know." His fist flicked into her gut.

Rosemary's universe dissolved into pinpoints of light and the contents of her stomach rose halfway up her throat. Gritting her teeth, she refused to say.

"Let's do this right," Chaco said, stepping back. "Each of you take an arm and boost her up."

Garvey and Kicking Bull complied. Rosemary sagged between them, too dazed to stand on her own legs. Nausea assailed her, and it was a wonder she didn't pass out.

"Now, then," Chaco said, sliding his knife from its sheath. "Unless you want to lose your nose, you'll explain how it is you're riding Gault's animal."

"I don't know any Gault," Rosemary lied, and was rewarded with a knee to the midriff that compounded her agony tenfold.

Chaco wagged the knife in tiny circles. "You're easy on the eyes, lady. I'd love to diddle you, but that won't stop me from carving you up so bad, your own mother wouldn't recognize you." He pressed the edge of the blade to her right nostril. "Last chance. Where's Gault Morton?"

Rosemary had always considered herself fairly brave, but now she wavered. *Mutilation.* The word pealed in her head like the toll of doom. She found herself questioning whether the loss of her nose was worth her continued silence. Then she thought of Sam and Eddy, and her faltering courage solidified into a solid granite wall of resistance. "Go to hell."

Chaco sneered and tensed his knife arm. "Try to be reasonable with some people, and look at how they treat you. It's your decision. After today you'll never look at yourself in the mirror again."

Rosemary braced for the moment of truth.

Suddenly Chaco glanced up, past her, and shock spread across his scarred countenance—shock mixed with more than a little fear. Hooves hammered, and something struck Garvey Morton from behind and sent him sprawling. Kicking Bull released her and spun, but he was too slow. A rifle stock smashed into his temple and he fell in his tracks, oozing blood.

That left Chaco, who frantically backpedaled while clawing at one of his pistols. There was a blur of movement and a black battering ram slammed into him, catapulting him head over heels. He did not rise when he finally came to rest.

Garvey did, though. Bellowing like a bull elk in rut, he heaved erect. A moccasin flashed and connected with his face, turning his legs to mush. He melted to the grass and lay twitching like someone afflicted with a nervous condition.

Nate King was the living embodiment of raw fury. Reining his bay around, he leaped down and gripped her by the shoulders. "Are you hurt? Where did these polecats come from? And what are you doing so far from the wagon?"

Breathlessly, briefly, Rosemary explained. She left out mentioning the money in her pouch and how it got there, and ended with "Where *were* you? We expected you back a couple of hours ago."

"Your ox strayed farther than I reckoned."

The animal was behind her, the lead rope left where King had dropped it. "Jeremiah!" Rosemary exclaimed, but the animal no more knew its name than it did genuine affection. To the mountain man she said, "Thank God you came when you did. But what do we do with these scoundrels?"

"What else is there to do?" King trained his Hawken on Garvey Morton and cocked the hammer.

Never in a million years would Rosemary have thought he could kill someone in cold blood. "You'd shoot them when they're unconscious and can't defend themselves?"

"You couldn't defend yourself, and they were about to do a lot worse to you. If we don't turn them into maggot bait, they won't rest until they've done the same to us. Is that what you want?"

"There has to be another way," Rosemary said. There had to be more to frontier life than the incessant killing, killing, killing.

"Not unless you want to tie them up and hold them prisoner until the cows come home," King said in complete jest.

Rosemary grasped at the straw. "I like that idea. That's what we'll do. Bind them and haul them to the wagon. We can decide how to deal with them later."

"You're serious?" Nate King said, and when she nodded, he sighed and shook his head in disbelief. "I'll go along this once. But you're making a mistake. Men like these see mercy as a weakness, and compassion as stupid. They'll kill you the first chance they get."

"Then we won't give them that chance," Rosemary said optimistically.

The mountain man took a coil of rope from his saddle and bound the three men with their wrists behind their backs. He also relieved them of their pistols and knives and flung the weapons in among the trees. Giving each of their rifles the same treatment, he remarked, "When you clip a painter's claws, it's less apt to scratch you."

"How will they survive if we let them go?"

"Who cares?" King rejoined. "I've met Chaco and the Morton brothers before. Years ago, at the last of the rendezvous. They were snakes in the grass then, and they still have more scales than a rattler. The world would be better off without them."

"But it's not right for us to set ourselves up as their judge, jury, and executioners," Rosemary said. " 'Vengeance is mine, sayeth the Lord.' "

"You can quote Scripture until doomsday and it won't change the fact that these men are vermin. Let them live, and the next lives they take will be on your head."

Rosemary hadn't thought of that. "I need time to think," she said. "I've never murdered anyone before."

"Killing isn't murder when you're killing murderers," King rebutted. "They shoot mad dogs, don't they?"

Rosemary resorted to the last argument of her gender when men were being stubborn. "Please. Do it for me."

Sam and Eddy were anxiously awaiting them, and their happiness at seeing Nate King was unbounded.

Gault didn't share their sentiments. "You!" he barked as King reined to a stop, and coldly regarded the three limp forms slumped over the other horses. "I'd never have believed there was a coon alive who could take all of them at once."

The mountain man dismounted and dumped Chaco, Garvey, and Kicking Bull onto the ground. "You and your brother haven't changed any, have you?"

"Why should we?" Gault said smugly. "We do right fine nowadays. We lay low near the trail, and when the Sioux are done, we take their leavings. Nothing illegal in that. And now we've got pretty near fifteen thousand dollars cached along the Platte where no one will ever find it."

"You're lucky the Sioux never discovered you," Rosemary said.

Gault's gaze drifted beyond her, and he abruptly surged upward but couldn't rise more than an inch. "Damn you, woman. Thanks to you, our luck just ran out!"

Rosemary smiled knowingly. "I'm not about to fall for the same trick twice."

"He's telling the truth, Ma," Eddy said, snatching at her dress to get her attention. "There's an Indian yonder, watching us."

Rosemary turned, and to her dismay spied a lone Sioux on horseback off under the trees. They were so preoccupied, he had approached within forty yards unseen. His face was hid in shadow, but she swore she could feel his gaze upon her.

"I'll drop him!" Sam yelled, his rifle rising.

Nate King was quicker. Grabbing the barrel, he pushed the rifle aside, bawling, "Don't shoot!"

"Why the blazes not?" Sam sought to pull loose, but he was no match for the mountain man's steely sinews. "He's a hostile. Him and his kind massacred our friends, and he'll do the same to us."

"You're only guessing he took part," King said, refusing to relinquish the gun. "He might not have."

"But he'll let the war party know where we are," Sam protested. "We'll have the whole Sioux nation down on our heads."

Rosemary agreed. She elevated her own rifle, but the

Sioux had magically vanished. "Where did he go?" she asked, perplexed.

Sam was a study in frustration. "He's gone, and it's all your fault!" he railed at Nate King. "You should have let me put a window in his skull while I had the chance."

Support came from an unlikely source. "The boy's right," Gault Morton declared. "We're as good as dead. Cut me free so I can go down fighting."

Eddy's fingers were still entwined in Rosemary's dress. "Are we going to be scalped, Ma?"

Rosemary stared at the mountain man in silent reproach. Had her trust in him been misplaced? He had saved her back on the trail, but by sparing the Sioux warrior he might have sealed their fates. "Of course not," she responded, hoping she sounded more confident than she felt. To Nate King she said, "What now?"

"We get out of here." The mountain man had been surveying the surrounding countryside, but now he turned and read in their faces what was in their hearts. "All of you think we should have killed him, I take it? But what if the war party is close enough to hear the shot? They'll be on us in minutes. This way, he has to go find them We've bought ourselves extra time."

"Where do you suggest we go?" Rosemary inquired. "Off somewhere to hide until the next wagon train comes along?"

"I suggest we head for Fort La Ramie. It shouldn't take more than four or five days. You'll be safe there, and there might be mules or oxen for sale."

Rosemary remembered Harry Trapp talking about the post. It had been built back in '34 on a bank of the Laramie River about a mile above the Laramie's junction with the Platte, and was named after a French trapper, Jacques La Ramie, who was ambushed and slain by Arapahos in that general area. A trading post, it thrived during the trapping era but fell on hard times when the beaver trade ended. Then emigrants began flocking west

121

along the Oregon Trail, and now Fort Laramie was a favorite stopover on the route to South Pass. According to Harry Trapp, there was a rumor the Army was considering buying it and turning the post into a military installation for the express purpose of protecting westbound pioneers. "They have livestock for sale?"

"Now and then emigrants trade extra animals for provisions," King said. "Or sell them for a little extra spending money."

Sam wasn't satisfied with the idea. "What about our three oxen? The Sioux will use them for target practice, then burn our wagon and all our effects. I say we stay."

"We'll take your oxen with us," King proposed. "As for your effects, I'm sorry. You can only take what your horses can carry."

Gault had been listening with keen interest. "Wait a minute. They don't own any horses."

The mountain man smiled. "They do now."

"You rotten son of a bitch," Gault snarled. "You're fixing to steal ours and leave us trussed like pigs for the slaughter."

"I couldn't have put it better myself."

Swearing a mean streak, Gault tried to kick King in the shins, but his leg didn't quite reach far enough. "Damn your hide! You know what the Sioux will do to us." Gault was scared and made no attempt to hide it. "What about you, lady?" he appealed to Rosemary. "Can you ride off and leave fellow whites to be tortured alive?"

"After how you treated me, dare you ask?" was Rosemary's rejoinder.

"Let bygones be bygones," Gault pleaded. "My pards and me will go our own way and forget we ever set eyes on you. We'll also forget about the ton of money you're toting."

"Money?" Nate King said.

Her ears burning, Rosemary couldn't get her tongue to work.

Gault glanced from her to King and back again. "He doesn't know you helped yourself to all the pokes those pilgrims were carrying?"

Steeling herself, Rosemary glanced at Nate King and said in her defense, "It's not as if they had any use for it. I have two boys to provide for. I did what I thought best."

"I don't blame you," King responded, and stared at Sam. "You must have enough to buy a new wagon and whatever else you'll need. So there's really no reason to stay here, is there?"

Rosemary realized his annoyance was directed at her eldest, not at her. To prevent Sam from sassing off, she instructed him to fetch the rest of their ammunition, then told Eddy to bring their jerky.

Nate King dragged Garvey, Kicking Bull, and Chaco over next to Gault. "When they come around, tell them this is for Sam Williams."

"Who?" Rosemary said.

"An old trapper who lived in the Green River country. He loved the mountains and stayed on after most trappers had gone east. A friendlier soul you couldn't meet. He was always willing to share his food and spare blankets with anyone who happened by." King paused. "One day a friend of mine by the name of Shakespeare McNair stopped to see him. Old Sam had been murdered. Shot in the back while standing at his stove. His cabin had been ransacked and all the furniture smashed."

Rosemary glanced at Gault, who was shamming an interest in the clouds. "And you suspect these four are to blame?"

"I know they were. They were seen in the area a few days before it happened. And McNair found the tracks of four horses leading from the old man's cabin. Three were shod, one wasn't."

"So?" Gault sneered. "It doesn't prove we were responsible. Anyway, we had nothing against that old coot. Why would we kill him?"

"Because of the rumor," King said. "Old Sam was supposed to have several thousand dollars squirreled away from his trapping days. It wasn't true, though. You and your friends killed him for nothing." King took a coil of rope from Garvey's horse, drew his Bowie, and cut four equal lengths about fifteen inches long.

"What are those for?" Gault wanted to know.

"Your ankles."

Gault unleashed the worst torrent of profanity yet, blistering the very air with his curses. As King went from one prone figure to the next, Gault strained to snap his bounds. When his turn came, he kicked and bucked and snarled like a beast gone berserk.

Lunging, King slammed his knees down onto Gault's legs, leaving Gault with no recourse but to submit to having them tied.

"I hope to God the Sioux get their hands on you, Grizzly Killer. I hope they cut off your oysters and make you eat them."

Rosemary climbed into the Conestoga after sets of spare clothes for her and the boys. Nearly every article had its attendant memory; the rocking chair Bert made for her, the quilt her mother labored over for years, tools that belonged to her father, her prized maple chest of drawers, and more, so much more. She gathered what little jewelry she had and a few small keepsakes.

The mountain man had fashioned lead ropes for the oxen. He gave one to Rosemary, the other to Sam. King mounted the bay, and with him in the lead, they rode toward the Oregon Trail.

Her emotions in upheaval, Rosemary repeatedly glanced back. The Conestoga had been more than a means of transportation. It was a symbol of her family's new life in the Promised Land. She couldn't bear to think she would never see it, or all her possessions, ever again.

Rosemary bestowed a last glance on the mound of fresh earth that covered the man she had loved, heart and soul. In their haste they had neglected to erect an appropriate marker. A board with his name or a wooden cross would do. She went to rein up.

"Ma!" Eddy exclaimed, pointing westward. "Do you see what I see?"

Rosemary shifted, and blinked. As if the Sioux and the grizzly hadn't been enough, now Nature itself was rising up against them. "I see it," she marveled, her scalp prickling with foreboding. "God help us, I see it."

Chapter Ten

One night, shortly after the wagon train began its odyssey, one of the emigrants had asked Harry Trapp which he feared most, Indians or wild animals. The pilot had chuckled and replied it was neither. "The thing I fear worst, more than having my hair lifted by the Blackfeet or my skull crushed by an ornery griz, are the storms."

"Don't tell us you're afraid of a little thunder and lightning," someone joked.

Trapp let the laughter subside, then said, "I'm not talking about the kind of storms you're used to, friend. They're puny compared to storms out here. Imagine winds strong enough to blow a wagon over. Lightning bolts that rain down like hail. And thunder that can burst your eardrums." Trapp had stopped to fiddle with the fire. "I don't blame you if you're skeptical. But I've seen them. I've lived through them. And I pray to God we don't run into one."

Rosemary had dismissed it as another of Trapp's tall

tales, like the one about buffalo herds over a million strong. But now, as she gaped at the colossal thunderhead to the west, she realized that if Trapp were still alive, she would owe him an apology.

A storm front was moving in. But what a front! A roiling cauldron of ominous dark clouds rose miles high into the atmosphere, clouds that writhed and coiled as if alive. Half the sky was blotted out and the prairie underneath cast into preternatural night. Throughout the thunderhead danced flashing lights, and from deep within its bowels rumbled continuous thunder, although Rosemary saw no lightning as yet. "Mr. King!" she called out.

"I see it," the mountain man replied as nonchalantly as if she were calling his attention to an antelope.

"Shouldn't we take cover? Or maybe go back and ride the storm out in the Conestoga?"

"It's a long ways off yet. We can cover a lot of ground before it hits."

Rosemary swallowed a protest and rode on. She had to keep reminding herself he knew best. To him the wilderness was home, and if anyone could see them safely through to Fort Laramie, it was he.

Soon the wind picked up. The tops of the trees swayed, then the middle boughs, and finally those lower down. Rosemary felt a brisk, moist sensation on her face, not unpleasant after the heat of the day. Her hair streamed behind her, her bangs whipping in the steadily increasing gusts.

The eastern half of the sky grew darker. Sinuous tendrils from the main mass were spreading outward like the tentacles of a gigantic octopus, swallowing all the blue in their path. And all the while, the rumbling grew louder and the moisture in the air thickened until it could be sliced with a butter knife.

"I don't like this, Ma," Eddy said.

Rosemary was apprehensive, too, but Nate King

showed no sign of slowing anytime soon. He was making straight toward the onrushing juggernaut. Trying to act as indifferent as he for the benefit of her boys, she tugged on the lead rope to the ox she was leading.

Sam didn't share her confidence in the mountain man. "Are you sure this is the right thing to do, Mr. King?"

"We can't avoid it, so why fret?" was the mountain man's reply.

They couldn't skirt it, that was for sure, Rosemary agreed. The front stretched from the northern horizon to the southern horizon.

"We should be fine so long as there aren't any tornadoes," Nate King mentioned. "I was caught in one once, and it's not an experience I'd like to repeat."

Missourians saw twisters now and then. When Rosemary was seven or eight one struck a neighboring town, Linfield. Her father had driven over to see if they could be of help, and to this day she vividly recalled the terrible devastation. Three-fourths of the town had been destroyed, the buildings ripped apart as if they were so many sticks. Fourteen people had lost their lives, including a baby sucked from its mother's arms up into the funnel cloud. Dead and missing livestock had numbered in the hundreds, mostly cattle caught in the open by the half-mile-wide tornado.

"There but for the grace of God go us," her father had said, and Rosemary, watching the mother of the missing baby weep, had wondered what the woman had done to make God so mad at her.

A whistling sound ended Rosemary's childhood reminiscence. The wind was redoubling its assault on the trees. A hollow boom fell on her ears from out of the depths of the thunderhead, succeeded by a seemingly unending series, each louder than the one before. "How much longer before we stop?" she hollered to be heard above the din.

"A bit farther yet," the mountain man shouted back.

What Rosemary said next wasn't very ladylike, but she said it under her breath so no one else would hear.

Cottonwoods and willows were whipping and bending like reeds in a gale. The tall grass rippled and ebbed much like the surface of a hurricane-tossed sea. Rosemary saw a bird, a sparrow, she thought, try to take wing from out of a bush, only to be flung back into it as if by an unseen hand.

Eddy slowed, and when she came alongside him, he marshaled a feeble smile. "If that wind gets any stronger, it'll blow me right out of my saddle."

Rosemary rested a hand on his shoulder. "It won't be much longer. We need to put as much distance as we can between us and those Sioux."

"Even Indians wouldn't be out in weather like this," Eddy responded.

Out of the mouths of children, Rosemary reflected. Suddenly the wind intensified to a frightening degree, buffeting her so severely it nearly took her breath away. Tucking her chin low, she shouted, "Hold your head down, Edward, and it won't be so bad." His answer was whipped into distorted fragments, but he did as she had suggested.

A raindrop fell. Then another, and yet a third. The ox was dragging its hooves again, and Rosemary had to yank with all her might to convince it to keep moving.

Nate King halted, gestured at the trees, and yelled something lost to the wind. Flicking his reins, he entered the undergrowth. Sam slowed, verified that Rosemary and Edward were close behind, and followed King in.

The light had faded to a twilight gray and was diminishing rapidly by the second. Another minute and the seething mass of the thunderhead would be on top of them. Fearful that they had waited too long to seek cover, Rosemary rode in under the trees, Eddy's mount glued to hers. It was so dark that King and Sam were mere silhouettes, even though they weren't more than ten yards away.

Nate King swung down and hurriedly tied his bay and Jeremiah to a tree. "Secure your animals," he directed. "Then strip off your saddles and saddlebags."

More rain was falling. It wasn't a sustained drizzle yet, but it would be soon. Nature was on the verge of unleashing her full ferocity.

Rosemary deposited her saddle under the same bush where the mountain man had deposited his.

He led them to a thicket, where, to her surprise, he eased down onto his stomach and proceeded to wriggle in among the maze of thin branches, dragging his beaded parfleches in after him.

"I never would have thought of this," Sam said, and emulated the frontiersman's example.

Larger, harder drops spattered Rosemary's head and shoulders as she dropped onto her hands and knees. Peering into the thicket was like peering down a well; she couldn't see much of anything.

"What are you waiting for?" Nate King yelled. "A formal invite?"

Eddy scrambled past her. "Come on, Ma. We won't get as wet in here."

Against her better judgment Rosemary crawled in. A branch nicked her cheek. Another scratched her ear. There was plenty of space for a boy Eddy's age, but it was a tight fit for an adult. She adjusted her pouch so it wouldn't snag and pulled her saddlebags along by her fingertips. Above her the thicket rattled and shook. Few raindrops penetrated all the way. "Pretty smart idea," she said to herself.

"Thanks," came Nate King's reply from an arm's length to her right. "I learned it from Shakespeare McNair."

Rosemary could barely see his handsome face. "You've mentioned McNair before.

You sound quite fond of him."

"We've been through a lot together. He's always stuck be me, through thick and thin. As far as I'm concerned, he's the most decent man alive."

King said more, but he was drowned out by a thunderclap that shook the ground on which Rosemary lay. With elemental ferocity the storm broke. The wind shrieked, the rain fell in a driving deluge, while all around crackling bolts of lightning speared the earth with clockwork regularity. Chaos ruled, and caught under the thicket at the heart of the maelstrom, Rosemary Spencer covered her head with her arms and wished to God her family had never left Missouri.

The thicket shook in violent throes, the wind threatening to tear the growth out by the roots. A bolt of lightning seared a nearby tree, and Rosemary thought her eardrums would shatter from the blast of thunder that ensued.

Like feathers on a duck's back, the compact foliage and tightly spaced branches warded off the worst of the rain, but more and more drops made it through. She felt a trickle on her left shoulder and shifted so it would miss her, only to feel another trickle on her head. Again she moved, as far as the cramped confines permitted.

Another sizzling bolt from on high lit up the terrain as brightly as day. For a few seconds Rosemary saw her sons clearly. Sam was on his side, staring up at the tumultuous tempest in pure wonderment. Eddy was on his stomach with his arms over his head. Reaching out, she squeezed his shoulder. His eyes peeked out and she gave him a warm smile, which he reciprocated. Then the darkness closed in again, the storm waging war against the planet that spawned it.

The closest bolt of lightning yet flared like a Roman candle, and Rosemary thought she heard the squeal of a horse. She looked toward the trees where the animals were tied, but a black veil descended before she could spot them.

Rosemary lost all track of time. An hour might have gone by, or it might have been two, when the tempest suddenly stilled; the wind and the rain slackened and only a few random bolts of lightning lanced from the heavens. "It's over at last!" In her excitement she raised her head too quickly and a branch poked her in the temple.

"Not yet," Nate King informed her.

"But just listen," Rosemary said.

"The center of the storm is passing over us. The eye of the storm, some folks call it." King's face was almost ghostly in the gloom. "There's more to come."

"Of course there is," Rosemary quipped. The wilderness was indeed a harsh taskmaster. Raising her voice, she asked, "Boys, how are you holding up?"

"Just fine," Sam replied. "A little wet is all."

"I'm hungry, Ma," Eddy said. "Can I have a piece of jerky?"

Rosemary tried to bend to pull her saddlebags nearer, but there wasn't enough room.

"Afraid not, son. I can't quite get at it. You'll have to wait until this storm is over."

"Stupid storm," Eddy muttered.

As if taking umbrage at the insult, Nature renewed its onslaught with reborn fury. The rain, the wind, the lightning, pummeled the prairie mercilessly. Rosemary slid her right arm under her chin and closed her eyes. She wasn't afraid anymore. But she was ungodly tired. The lack of rest was catching up with her. She thought of Bert, of the day they became man and wife, and how handsome he had looked in his store-bought clothes, the only suit he ever owned. She missed him so much. He had been more than her husband; he had been the best friend she ever had. Sure, there were times they didn't get along all that well, times when they spatted more than they cuddled, times when she wanted to throttle the living daylights out of him. But by and large he was as good a man and as loyal a husband as any woman could ask for.

Rosemary wondered what Nate King's wife was like. Winona, wasn't that her name? She probably was a lot like most white women. Oh, she lived in a hide lodge, but when you got right down to it, was that so drastically different from living in a frame house? And was wearing buckskins all that different from wearing a cotton or wool dress? Rosemary wondered if Winona went on buffalo hunts with the braves. And whether Winona had ever lost any of her loved ones to enemy war parties. Rosemary would enjoy meeting her one day to talk over womanly matters and compare perspectives.

The dull rumble of thunder snapped Rosemary's eyes open. She had fallen asleep in the middle of the storm! More thunder pealed, but from off to the east, not overhead. The wind wasn't anywhere near as strong, and the rain had tapered to a light drizzle. "The worst must be over," she remarked.

"It is," Nate King answered. "Time we were moving on."

It was light enough for Rosemary to see him and her sons. The mountain man began to slide backward, his hands and elbows supplying the leverage, crawling out the way he had entered. "You heard the man, boys."

Shafts of sunlight were spearing through the clouds. The whole world glistened with a wet sheen, and drops pattered from every tree and bush. Rosemary arched her spine as she straightened, relieving a kink.

The woods resembled a battleground. Limbs had been torn from boles and lay scattered singly and in piles. Swatches of vegetation had been totally flattened. Puddles and pools that would soon seep underground were everywhere.

"Ma!" Sam bawled. "My horse is dead!"

That it was, along with an ox that had been tied to the

same lightning-scarred oak. The pair were sprawled close together, the ox's head split down the middle as if by an ax, the edges of its flesh charred black. The horse didn't have a mark on it. The rest of their mounts were fine, but the second of their three oxen had broken loose and gone off who-knew-where.

Nate King searched for tracks, but the rain had obliterated them. "It looks as if you're down to just one. I can go hunt for it, though, if you want."

"Why put yourself to so much bother?" Rosemary happily patted her pouch. "Like you said, I can buy an entire team now."

King stared a moment, his face inscrutable. "Can you and your youngest ride double? I'll take point, and Sam can bring up the rear."

"Sure," Rosemary said. Was it her imagination, or was he upset with her for taking the money? He hadn't said anything before.

The Oregon Trail was a trail of mud. The rain had filled the scores of ruts to overflowing, and the water had spread across the yards-wide bare earth exposed by the wear of thousands of wheels, hooves, and tramping feet. Every step the dun took resulted in a sucking sound.

Rosemary had hoped the storm front would bring cooler temperatures, but within half an hour it had to be well into the nineties. The moisture was evaporating rapidly, but not rapidly enough. The air was muggy. Impossibly humid. Her dress clung to her like a second skin, and she was constantly mopping her forehead with a sleeve.

Sam was in exceptionally fine spirits. He whistled "Turkey in the Straw" and tapped his saddle in time to the melody.

"What has you in such a good mood?" Rosemary asked.

"We've given those pesky hostiles the slip," Sam said.

"The storm erased our tracks, just like it did the ox's. They have no idea where we are."

Nate King overheard and shifted around. "You've got it backwards. They know exactly where we are. Whites use only this one trail. We might as well have bull's-eyes painted on our backs." He squinted skyward. "If they're after us, they'll catch up by sunset."

"What then?" Rosemary asked. "Do you speak their language? Can you convince them we're friendly?"

"I'm fluent in sign talk," the mountain man said, "but it won't do us a lick of good. The Sioux aren't fond of whites in general, and me in particular." He let out with a long sigh. "Some years back I had a run-in with one of their tribes and—"

"Tribes?" Sam interrupted. "How many are there?"

"The Lakota are divided into seven groups." King ticked them off on his fingers. "The Oglalas, the Brules, the Minneconjous, the Sans Arcs, the Hunkpapas, the Two Kettles, and the Blackfeet Sioux—"

Again Sam interrupted. "But I thought the Blackfeet are a whole separate tribe?"

"They are. The Blackfeet Sioux live at the north end of Sioux territory, between the rest of the Lakotas and the Blackfeet."

Rosemary perked up. "Which of them attacked the wagon train?"

"The Oglalas, the southernmost tribe. They're not as warlike as the Minneconjous or the Sans Arcs, but they don't like having the Oregon Trail through their country. If they could, they'd close it, permanently."

"So you were saying you had a run-in?" Rosemary prompted when King was silent a bit.

"The Minneconjou had my wife. I wanted her back."

"There must have been more to it than that."

"Some blood was shed. The Sioux have had it in for me ever since. I generally fight shy of them unless I have no other choice." King straightened in the saddle and gazed northward.

Out on the prairie black specks had appeared. Dozens upon dozens, roving slowly eastward. Rosemary couldn't quite tell what they were. "Are those antelope?"

"Buffalo."

"I'd love to see them up close." So far Rosemary had been denied the privilege. This, after the tales she'd heard about herds so vast they blotted out the plain. Herds miles long and miles wide. Herds that delayed wagon trains for a week or better. Yet these were the first buffalo she had seen the whole trip. She made a comment to that effect.

"This time of year the large herds have pushed on south toward Texas," Nate King revealed. "Be here in the spring and there will be so many you couldn't count them if you had a century."

Sam was interested in their discussion. "Is buffalo meat as tasty as everyone says? My grandfather swore it's better than beef and venison combined."

"It's good, but most mountaineers I've met swear painter meat is tastiest."

Rosemary knew of only two kinds of painters. The first used a brush and a canvas. The second had four legs and a tail. "You can't mean mountain lion?"

"Nothing but," King confirmed. "I've eaten some myself, and I'd stack it against the fanciest steak in the fanciest restaurant anywhere. One man I know would only eat painter meat and nothing but painter meat. Single-handed, he wiped out half the mountain lions in the central Rockies."

"And it never made him ill?" Rosemary wouldn't care if she were starving. She would never eat a mountain lion, and that was final. They were prone to a disease, the name of which eluded her but occasionally proved fatal to anyone who ate their tainted flesh.

"He only ate healthy painters and cooked the meat

until it was well done," King explained. "He'd still be eating cougars today if the Bloods hadn't spilled his brains all over a creek bed."

"How do you stand living with so much violence day in and day out?" Rosemary queried. "I couldn't. I prefer a peaceful life. I want to die of old age, like my grandmother did, sitting quietly in my rocking chair."

"You get used to it," King said. "When I first came west, I was as shocked as you. I thought that anyone who lived in the mountains must be crazy. Or crave an early grave. Then the truth hit me." He smiled wistfully, an Adonis in profile. "Life is violent by nature, a constant fight for survival. Animals are always killing one another. Birds eat worms, foxes eat rabbits, painters eat deer, bears eat anything and everything."

"But that's not the same kind of violence," Rosemary said. "They kill in order to eat. People kill for killing's sake."

"I used to think that, too, until I watched some red ants invade a colony of black ants. The reds wiped most of the black ants out and took the few that were left back to their own mound. To use as food or slaves, I reckon." King glanced back. "How are those ants any different from us?"

"Are you saying violence is ingrained into our natures?" Rosemary shook her head. "I refuse to accept that. There must be more to the human race. Look at Scripture. Our Maker created us in His own image. If what you claim is true, what does it say about God?"

"Is this the same God that let all your friends be slaughtered?" The mountain man pursed his lips. "I don't have all the answers. I only know there must be a purpose to the violence or there wouldn't be any."

Rosemary had to remember not to take their bearded deliverer at face value. On the surface he was as ordinary as they came, but underneath lurked layers within layers. A man of two worlds, at home in the wilderness and among his civilized brethren. Born in New York, he'd mentioned once. Yet, given his druthers, he had selected the wild spaces to the crowded streets of the city of cities. Only one man in a thousand would make the same decision. Make that one man in ten thousand.

Eddy's cheek was against her back, his arms around her waist. He hadn't spoken a word since they resumed their journey, and Rosemary assumed he was asleep. Not so. "Ma, can I tell you something?"

"Anything. A mother's ears are always open."

"I don't want to go to Oregon. I want to go back to our farm. I want to live just like we did before Pa got the notion to move."

"I'm sorry, son. It's not possible. We sold the farm, and I very much doubt Mr. Pringle will sell it back."

"Why not? We have a lot of money now, don't we?"

More money than they ever had, Rosemary reflected, her heart leaping at the idea. The only thing Harvey Pringle valued more than land was money. If she offered him two or three times the amount he paid, he just might go for it.

"Can we, Ma? Please?"

Rosemary recalled how much their new life in Oregon meant to Bert. How excited he had been. How he had lost his life in quest of his dream.

"Ma?"

"There comes a time, son, when we put the old behind us and take up the new. Our farm is gone. I miss it, and you miss it, but we have to look ahead to the future. Your father gave his life trying to provide us with a better life. It wouldn't be fair to his memory to give up. We have to see this through, if for no other reason than to prove your father didn't die in vain." Rosemary looked over her shoulder. "Do you understand?"

"I suppose we shouldn't let Pa down," Eddy said, downcast.

Sam nudged his mount closer. "Once we reach the

Promised Land, little brother, you'll feel better. The red-skins are friendly, and the only bears in the Willamette Valley are black bears. The grizzlies have been driven high up into the Cascade Mountains."

"I don't care about that stuff," Eddy responded. "What about the people?"

"Pa told me they're the friendliest folks you'd ever want to meet. Most are farming families, just like us "

"Are there any kids?"

Rosemary answered. "Enough to fill a one-room school, according to the letter your father received from the minister at a place called Eugene."

"School?" Eddy shriveled several inches. "Aw, shucks. The Promised Land isn't all it's cracked up to be."

Laughing, Rosemary faced around and discovered that Nate King had reined to the side of the trail and was gazing back the way they had come. She came to a stop beside him and wheeled her horse so she could probe the landscape without having to turn her head. "Is something wrong? You look as if you swallowed a bag of nails."

"Don't you see them?"

Rosemary's eyes narrowed to slits. The only evidence of life she saw were some birds. "See what?"

"The riders who are shadowing us."

Chapter Eleven

Whoever they were, they were crafty. They stayed far back and only made the mistake of momentarily showing themselves twice. The first time, Nate King had spotted them. The next, both King and Sam caught a fleeting glimpse. So fleeting, neither the mountain man nor Rosemary's oldest could tell who the riders were, or how many.

"They must be Sioux," Sam guessed. "The same war party that wiped out everyone else."

That made sense to Rosemary, but Nate King was scratching his beard and wore a quizzical look. "Do you agree?"

"Sioux usually wouldn't show themselves until they were right on top of us. It could be some young warriors who don't know any better and are hankering to lift hair."

"Should we make our stand here?" Rosemary asked.

The site was favorable. Both sides of the trail were flanked by oaks and heavy undergrowth.

"No, we'll push on until dark," King said, and clucked to the bay.

Now it was Rosemary who was puzzled. Kneeing her horse up next to his, she said, "Don't take this wrong, but I think you're making a mistake. We still have an hour of sunlight left. We should wait for them and finish it."

"In broad daylight? When we don't know exactly how many there are?" King chortled softly. "Why not tie ourselves to some trees and make it just as easy for them?"

Rosemary's temper surfaced. "I'm only trying to be helpful. It makes more sense for us to pick the time and the spot than to wait for them to spring an ambush."

"That it does," King said, and grinned. "You're learning, ma'am. Be patient awhile and we'll do just that."

His compliment didn't placate Rosemary one bit. "You have a plan? Why didn't you say so. I swear, you fluster me on purpose."

"It's been my experience women are born flustered and spend the rest of their lives letting everyone else know it."

Were Rosemary a man, she would have belted him in the mouth. "You think you're funny, don't you? Belittling me in front of my children? Treating me as if I'm a dunce."

"I was only trying to make you smile, Mrs. Spencer. You're too high-strung. You need to learn how to relax and enjoy life more."

"My husband has died, my children and I are stranded in this godforsaken prairie, we've lost almost all our worldly possessions, and a Sioux war party is out to kill us." Rosemary couldn't contain herself. *"What in hell is there for me to enjoy about any of this?"*

Nate King acquired a somber look. "I'm sorry. You're

right. It was thoughtless of me to try and cheer you up."
Flicking his reins, he rode ahead.

Rosemary's anger evaporated in a tide of self-reproach. She shouldn't have blown up at him like she did. He was only trying to help.

"That wasn't very nice of you, Ma," Eddy whispered.

A jab of Rosemary's heels brought her alongside the big bay once again. "I'm the one who should be sorry. I shouldn't have snapped at you. It was uncalled for."

"We're all a mite on edge," the mountain man said. "Don't be too hard on yourself. You're taking this better than most would."

"I have to," Rosemary responded, "for two obvious reasons."

Their eyes met, and Rosemary couldn't help thinking that if they had met under more pleasant circumstances, in another time and place—when they were both single—their lives might have taken a whole other course. Then the moment passed, and King was staring straight ahead. Rosemary's cheeks grew warm.

Presently, the blazing sun dipped to the western horizon. Low emerald hills appeared to the north and south, the first Rosemary had seen in ages. The Platte River twisted and turned every which way, meandering through a lowland valley rich with grass and abundant timber. Several deer took bounding flight at their approach, and a jay squawked at them from high atop a willow.

Nate King rode faster. "I've been this way quite a few times," he mentioned, "and there's a certain spot that's perfect for our purpose."

Ten more minutes brought them to a loop in the river. Hemmed by water on three sides and a bluff to the north was a grassy space wide enough for a large wagon train to circle. "Here we are," King announced. "This is where we'll make camp."

"Right out in the open?" Rosemary was dubious.

King nodded. "Smack in the middle. And we'll build a fire big enough to be seen for miles."

"Here you go again, confusing me."

They went about the business of picketing the horses, gathering firewood and water, and kindling a fire. Nate King instructed them to stay put and walked off into the thick growth flanking the bluff. Soon a pistol shot rang out, and when he returned, he was carrying a large rabbit.

Watching him skin and butcher it, Rosemary simmered in agitation and repeatedly glanced eastward. Finally she had to say something. "The Sioux were bound to hear that shot. They'll know exactly where we are, and can show up at any second."

King impaled a bloody piece of raw meat on a thin branch he had sharpened with his Bowie. "We have a couple of hours yet. They'll give us time to settle in so our guard will be down."

"Mr. Trapp told me the Sioux never attack at night," Sam mentioned.

"Ordinarily that's true," King said. "But I'm not so sure the riders we saw *are* Sioux."

Rosemary had another of her premonitions. "Who else would they be?" she asked.

King merely winked and aligned more meat onto the makeshift spit.

She must be wrong, Rosemary told herself. It couldn't be *them.* Rotating on her heels so she faced east, she engaged in small talk with her boys. Eddy was still in the doldrums and needed more cheering. She rambled on about their new life in Oregon, about the fine house they would have and the crops they could grow on their one hundred and sixty acres. "The first couple of years we can hire a hand for the work we can't do ourselves," she mentioned. Plowing required a man's strength. Samuel was big for his age, but he wasn't strong enough yet to work a plow a solid day through.

Nate King had put coffee on to brew. Sitting back, he licked a forefinger and raised it aloft.

"What are you doing?" Rosemary had to know.

"Testing the breeze. We want our friends down the trail to catch a whiff of our meal." King removed the spit from the fire. The meat was browned to a turn and dripping juices. "Eat hearty. It will be a long, cold night if they don't take the bait."

Rosemary took that to mean he intended to put out the fire when they turned in, a prudent step. Famished, she accepted a hot chunk of rabbit. Greasy fat smeared her fingers and dribbled down her chin, but she didn't mind. Once, her sloppy manners would have scandalized her. But now she went on eating. She refused to be concerned over something so trivial.

It was interesting, Rosemary mused, how a person's outlook changed with their circumstances. On the farm she had insisted everyone wash their hands before each meal, and on sterling behavior at the dinner table. Why, she had made Sam go to his room without supper once for having dirt under his fingernails! How silly she had been.

Nate King was rummaging in one of his parfleches. "I have a surprise for you, boy," he said to Eddy. "I bought it for a friend of mine named Kendall, who has a sweet tooth. But he won't mind sharing." King held out a small package sealed with a ribbon, such as was commonly done by clerks in general stores. Setting it on his knees, he untied the knot, delved his fingers under the paper, and held out a couple of pieces of hard candy.

"Gosh," Eddy declared, and glanced up hopefully. "Is it all right, Ma?"

"Certainly," Rosemary said rather gruffly. She was a stickler for eating healthfully and refused to let her sons gorge on sweets and cakes and pies, like some mothers were wont to do. "Help yourself."

King offered a piece to Sam, who accepted, and to

Rosemary, who refused. "There's more if you change your mind," he said, and plopped the piece into his own mouth. Then, draping his big arms across his legs, he leaned toward them. "Pay close attention. We're about to lay a trap for the polecats who have been following us. If you don't do exactly as I tell you, we could wind up dead."

"What do you want us to do?" Sam asked, eager to take part.

King sent the boys to collect brush while he spread blankets and saddles around the fire. When Sam and Eddy came back, he shoved their armfuls under one of the blankets. Seven more trips were required before he had enough. "That should do it," he said, stepping back.

From a distance it would appear the four of them were sound asleep.

The mountain man added wood to the fire, enough so it would burn another hour, possibly longer. After a last survey, he snatched up his Hawken and swung northward. "Follow me."

Rosemary's blood was racing. She let the boys go ahead of her and was careful not to lose sight of them. The dusky outline of the bluff reared against the sky, and King bore to the right to a well-defined game trail. How he knew it was there, Rosemary couldn't begin to guess. The higher they climbed, the steeper the slope became. Near the top she had to stoop over and use her free hand for added support.

King guided them to the crest overlooking their camp. "This will do just fine."

Rosemary bent her head back to admire the magnificent celestial spectacle. So many stars, they took her breath away. In contrast, the countryside around them was plunged in impenetrable darkness. Only their fire glowed bright, a lone beacon in the blanket of night.

The frontiersman sank onto his haunches, crossed his

legs, rested his right elbow on his knee, and sighted down his Hawken.

"What are you aiming at, Mr. King?" Sam asked.

"The campfire," King said. "I peg it at sixty yards, maybe a hair more." He motioned. "Make yourselves comfortable. We'll be here a spell."

Rosemary sat on the mountain man's right, Sam and Eddy on his left. She raised her own rifle and centered the bead on the fire. A long shot, but well within the rifle's limits. She could see their blankets and the horses and ox quite clearly. But no one could see them, mantled in gloom as they were.

Sam was practicing his aim, too. "I get it. We're going to pick them off when they close in."

"That we are," Nate King said. "But no one is to fire until I say so. Savvy?"

Nodding, Sam chuckled. "You're tricky, Mr. King. I like that. Pa always said a man should fight with his brain and not rely so much on brawn."

King endeared himself to Rosemary even more than he already had by saying, "Your father was a wise coon, son. Do him proud and grow up to be just like him."

Eddy fingered his rifle and gnawed on his lower lip. "I don't know if I can shoot this far," he said. "On our farm, I only shot targets at twenty paces or so."

"Then we'll keep your rifle in reserve," King said. "Be ready to hand it to me when I ask for it."

A disquieting notion occurred to Rosemary and she stared with sober misgivings at her sons. " 'Thou Shalt Not Kill,' " she quoted softly.

The mountain man's broad shoulders stiffened and he slowly faced her. "None of you? Ever?"

"We're farmers, Mr. King. We shoot game and kill chickens and a hog now and then, but we've never shot a living soul. I trust you realize what you're asking of us."

For a while the only sound was the whisper of the wind

and the distant yip of coyotes. Then Nate King said, "No one is to shoot but me. Pass your rifles to me in turn, starting with Rose, and reload when I hand you an empty."

It was the first time he had called her by her first name, and Rosemary's ears tingled. "Thank you," she said huskily.

Sam, however, wasn't anywhere near as pleased. "What's wrong with me shooting one of them? I don't mind killing."

"An eye for an eye, is that it?" Rosemary said, unsettled. "Do you want the death of another person on your conscience for the rest of your life?"

"Listen to your mother," King rallied to her cause. "Taking a human life isn't to be taken lightly. There's no going back. I've done it, but only when I had to."

"We have to now," Sam said, "or we'll be rubbed out." He appealed to Rosemary. "Won't you reconsider, Ma? There might be too many for Mr. King to drop by his lonesome. He'll need my help."

"I'm sorry, Samuel."

Sam wasn't done arguing. He opened his mouth—and was promptly silenced by the mountain man's big hand thrust over the lower half of his face.

"Quiet!" Nate King whispered. "Company has come calling."

The circle of firelight had acquired a two-legged moth flitting about its edges as soundlessly as a specter. As Rosemary looked on, the stalker edged into the open, a pistol in each hand. The slight stature, the wiry build, the raccoon hat, and the ferretlike bob of the man's head left no doubt who it was. "Chaco! But how?"

"If you meet in the next life, ask him," Nate King said, and took a deliberate bead. His forefinger curled around the trigger, his thumb around the hammer.

Pausing every few steps, Chaco slunk toward their blankets like a cat slinking toward mice.

Rosemary tensed for the blast of King's Hawken. Precious seconds elapsed. In another five or six strides Chaco would discover their ruse. "What are you waiting for?" she nervously asked.

"I saw three riders," King whispered. "I want them all in the light when I fire."

Chaco had stopped and was suspiciously studying the nearest blanket. He glanced toward the horses, then swiveled toward the bluff.

"He's figured it out!" Rosemary exclaimed. "He knows where we are."

"That's impossible," Nate King said. "He wouldn't look this way unless—" Suddenly he heaved erect and whirled.

Rosemary leaped up, too, and in doing so, she blundered into the path of King's rifle, which was swinging in a tight arc toward a matching pair of giant forms who had crept up on them undetected. She saw twin muzzles trained on them, saw twin grins crease the unkempt beards of the hulking Morton brothers.

"Not another twitch, mountain man!" Gault Morton barked.

"Not unless you want us to make wolf bait of the woman and her brats," Garvey Morton echoed.

Rosemary didn't blame Nate King for freezing. He might get one, but the other would surely drop her or one of the boys. "Don't fire!" she cried. "We'll do as you say."

"Like hell we will!" Sam surged up off the ground, pivoting and aiming in the blink of an eye. As fast as he was, the crack of his rifle came a split second after the crack of Gault Morton's.

Unadulterated horror coursed through Rosemary as her son was jolted backward by the heavy slug. Sam tottered on the rim, his arms pinwheeling. Nate King sprang, an arm outstretched, but his fingers missed their hold and Sam went over the edge in a swirl of dust.

A cry of utter anguish was torn from Rosemary's throat, a cry such as only a mother could voice. She bounded to the brink and peered over, but the brush that grew out from the cliff obstructed her view of the bottom.

"Back away from there, lady, or you can follow him down." Gault had drawn a pistol and both brothers were cautiously advancing.

Rosemary spun, her temples pounding from red-hot rage. Forgetting herself, forgetting she was armed with a rifle and had a pistol at her waist, she shrieked like a wildcat and threw herself at her son's murderer. Surprise slowed Gault's reaction. He hiked his arm to club her, but she was on him before the blow could descend, raking his face and neck with her nails. Only vaguely was she aware of a rush of movement to her left, of the boom of a rifle and the sounds of a struggle. Her whole being was focused on Gault Morton. On the scum she was going to kill for killing her son. The next swing of her right arm nearly blinded him, leaving bloody furrows in its wake.

"Damn you, bitch!"

A fist clipped Rosemary's left cheek and rocked her on her heels, but her fury propelled her forward again. Gault dwarfed her, yet she tore into him like a terrier into a wild boar. Clamping both hands onto his throat, she sank her fingernails in as deep as they would go. It evoked a howl of pain. Gault thrashed right and left, seeking to tear her off, but Rosemary clung on, feeling a damp sensation between her fingers and on her palms. Something—Gault's pistol, maybe—whisked toward her head and she received a jarring blow. Her vision blurred and her knees buckled. A callused hand was pressed against her face and she was shoved to the ground.

Rosemary braced for the blast of a shot, for the searing impact of a lead ball. Instead she heard muttered oaths and the pad of footfalls receding into the darkness.

Strong hands gripped her by the shoulders and she was aided to her feet.

Nate King swiped a bang from her eyes and asked, "How bad are you hurt?"

"My head," Rosemary said, touching the goose egg.

"Stay with Eddy," King said. Drawing a pistol, he spun and sped after Gault Morton. Within moments he was out of sight.

The mention of her youngest reminded Rosemary of her oldest's fate. Fighting dizziness and nausea, she turned. Eddy was gaping at the prone form of Garvey Morton. Rosemary stumbled closer, afraid the killer would rise up and attack them. She should have known better. She should have known Nate King wouldn't have left them if there was any chance of that happening.

Garvey Morton was dead. He had been shot high in the chest, but the bullet wound hadn't ended his vile life. King's Bowie had that honor. The hilt jutted from just below Garvey's sternum; the blade was completely buried. Copious amounts of blood flowed, forming a pool under the body.

"Edward?" Rosemary croaked. Her throat was dry and her lips felt stiff. She extended her arms and he ran into them, wrapping his own around her legs.

"Take me home, Ma! Please take me home!"

"Would that I could," Rosemary said tenderly, running her bloody fingers through his hair.

"First Pa, now Sam. I hate this awful prairie! Hate it! Hate it! Hate it!"

Rosemary's dizziness was almost gone, but her head was pounding fiercely, so much so, she could barely think. "Fetch my rifle," she directed. "We're going to find your brother."

"Do we have to, Ma?" Eddy balked. "I didn't like seeing Pa dead. I don't want to see Sam dead, too."

"Do it." Rosemary glanced down at her waist to verify that her pistol was still wedged under her belt. The simple movement lanced more agony through her skull. Her legs weakened and she staggered, then bit her lip so as not to cry out.

"Ma?" Eddy said anxiously.

His small hand found hers, and Rosemary leaned on him until the hammering eased to a manageable level and she could straighten. "Lead the way down," she said, accepting her rifle. "Go slow so I can keep up with you."

"Shouldn't we wait for Mr. King?"

"There's no telling how long he'll be." Rosemary had to find Sam, had to know for sure one way or the other. With the rifle to help steady her, she shuffled to the game trail. The steep incline daunted her. Her teeth clamped against the anguish, she eased onto her backside and slid down until they were midway to the bottom, where it was level enough to stand. As she rose, a gun boomed to the northwest.

Eddy gazed toward the ring of hills. "Mr. King is still after that fella."

"Let's hope he kills the son of a bitch."

"Ma!" Eddy declared, appalled. "What you just said!"

Rosemary stopped short and pressed a hand to her pounding head. "I'm sorry, son." He had never heard her swear. None of her family had. At an early age her mother had impressed on her that there were three things a woman never did: "Never talk to strangers, never let anyone know your true feelings, and never use foul language." The second taboo had always perplexed her, but her mother swore it was in her own best interests.

Now, with Eddy's eyes as wide around as walnuts, Rosemary said contritely, "It was unseemly of me, I know. But I'm only human. Women get mad, just like men do. And I'm powerful mad at what happened to your brother."

"I understand," Eddy responded. "Sometimes I feel

like cussing, too. But Pa always said he'd take a hickory switch to me if I did."

They continued lower. As they neared the bottom, Rosemary scoured the tall grass.

Eddy hurried ahead. "Where is he? I don't see him."

Neither did Rosemary. "Wait for me," she said, but her youngest wasn't about to slow down. To the northwest another shot shattered the stillness, farther off this time. Suddenly Rosemary remembered the third cutthroat, Chaco. She turned toward their camp, but he had vanished. Good riddance, she thought, and moved into pitch-black shadow at the base of the bluff. "Edward?"

"Over here, Ma. I still can't find Sam anywhere."

Rosemary moved toward him. "Keep talking so I can find you." She couldn't see more than a yard in front of her, if that.

"I'm close to the cliff. There's a lot of brambles and bushes."

That there was, more than Rosemary realized. She nearly bumped into Eddy, and together they roved blindly through the brush, twigs crackling underfoot, limbs snapping to the passage of their bodies. Halting, Rosemary craned her neck and tried to pinpoint exactly where Sam had gone over the edge. She thought it had been more to their left, so she pushed on for fifteen feet or more, without result.

"Too bad we don't have a lantern or a torch," Eddy said.

"Or a brand from the fire." Tugging on his sleeve, Rosemary led him toward their camp. She nearly tripped over her own feet when her youngest abruptly stopped and pivoted.

"Did you hear something, Ma?"

"Like what?"

"A moan."

"No, son, I didn't." Rosemary listened, and when the

sound wasn't repeated, she chalked it up to wishful thinking or a trick of the wind.

The horses all had their heads high and their ears pricked. Rosemary debated whether to conduct the search on horseback and dismissed the idea as impractical. Hunkering by the fire, she selected the unlit end of a thick branch and carefully pulled it from the flames. "This one is yours." She gave it to Edward.

Rosemary sidled to the right, seeking another suitable brand. Most of the firewood was burned completely through. She had to poke and prod with her rifle before she spied another thick piece that would do.

"Ma?" Eddy said.

"Just a moment." Rosemary gripped the brand and yanked it out. Spikes of flame nearly singed her fingers, and she stepped back to avoid being burned. "What is it?"

Eddy was pointing to their left, his features mirroring unbridled dread.

Her gut balling into a knot, Rosemary whirled, but she was already covered by two pistols.

"We meet again, bitch," Chaco leered. "Did you miss me?"

Chapter Twelve

Rosemary Spencer had never thought of herself as particularly brave. Life on the farm had been simple and peaceful, the way she liked her life to be. The only danger she had ever been in was the time one of the plow horses was frightened by a snake and reared, and she nearly had her head stove in by a flailing hoof.

In the past few days Rosemary had confronted more perils than in all the previous years of her life combined. She had encountered a marauding bear, eluded a Sioux war party, and escaped the clutches of a pack of human wolves. In the process she had learned a lot about herself. She had learned she possessed more backbone than she had given herself credit for, and when she had to, she could stand up to anyone or anything.

So when Chaco leered and extended his pistols, Rosemary smiled and said mockingly, "How proud you must be. It isn't every man who can gun down a woman and a child."

Her barb nettled him. "It takes more sand than you'd guess, lady," Chaco snapped. "But you can rest easy a while yet. I'll wait to dispose of you until Gault and Garvey get here."

"You've got a long wait, then," Rosemary said defiantly. "Garvey is dead and Nate King is after Gault as we speak."

Chaco hissed like a sidewinder, his swarthy countenance clouding. "That damned mountain man again! He almost got us killed by the stinking Sioux. Now this."

"How *did* you get away?" Rosemary asked, as much out of curiosity as to stall in the hope Nate King would show up.

"Thank the storm." Walking up to her, Chaco shoved one of his pistols under his belt and relieved her of her rifle and her own pistol. He threw them beyond the circle of firelight, then did likewise with Eddy's weapons.

"How did the storm help?" Rosemary prodded when it became apparent he wasn't going to elaborate.

"All that rain," Chaco absently answered while backing toward the horses. "It made our wrists all wet and slippery. I worked myself loose first and freed the rest." Without taking his eyes off her, he squatted to undo the picket rope.

"How did you get your guns back?" Rosemary asked, her hope fading. That last gunshot had been a long way off. King couldn't possibly get there in time to prevent whatever Chaco had in mind.

"We searched near where the mountain man jumped us. Kicking Bull figured that was where we'd find our guns, and sure enough, he was right."

Rosemary had forgotten about the fourth member of the vicious quartet. "Where is your Indian friend, anyway?"

"Wherever Injuns go to when they die." Chaco started leading the horses toward them. "The Happy Hunting Ground, or some nonsense like that." He wagged a pistol. "Climb on the pinto, lady. Your son can ride the mare. I'll take the dun."

Rosemary fiddled with the dun's bridle, buying yet more time. "How did your friend die?"

"How else? The Sioux. A passel of them came riding up, and we blew half off their horses before they knew what hit them. The rest skedaddled, but one put an arrow through Kicking Bull." Chaco vaulted astride the dun. "We caught three of their animals, and here we are. Only now we have our own horses back, and I have you and your boy as hostages." A thought seemed to strike him. "Where's your other kid? The older one Gault told me about?"

"Gault shot him."

Chaco stared, reading her expression. "Damn me if you're not telling the truth. Don't take it so hard, though. Pretty soon you and your other brat will join him." He gestured westward. "Light a shuck. And no tricks, or I'll splatter your son's brains all over creation."

Rosemary believed him. With a last longing glance at the bluff, she reined the pinto toward the Oregon Trail. Eddy followed. Chaco came last, a pistol in his left hand.

Until that moment Rosemary had not let herself feel the full effect of losing Samuel. She had been able to block it from her mind. But now, with Stygian gloom on all sides and nothing to occupy her but fear for her youngest's welfare, she succumbed to a seething whirlpool of bubbling emotion. First her beloved Bert, now her first-born. She tried not to cry, she truly did, but her heart wasn't to be denied its outlet. Tears flowed, and her throat became congested.

Rosemary wept silently. She refused to show weakness in front of Chaco. He would use it as an excuse to taunt her, or gloat at Sam's expense.

In due course her tears ebbed, and Rosemary wiped her cheeks with the back of her left hand, then checked on Eddy. He was slouched over, in the grip of deep despair. Smiling to cheer him, she said, "Two bits for your thoughts."

"It's supposed to be a penny, Ma," her boy said glumly.

"You're my son. You're worth the extra money."

Eddy's teeth gleamed. "I love you. You're the best mother a kid could have. You're always there for us when we need you."

"Always."

Chaco snickered in contempt. "Listen to you two simpletons. You're enough to give me indigestion. Keep your mouths shut until we get to where we're going."

"And where would that be?" Rosemary inquired, paying his threat no heed.

"A spot up yonder." Chaco peered toward the hills. "If Gault gives King the slip, he'll know to meet me there. And if that miserable mountain man comes after us, we'll dry-gulch the bastard. After we tend to you, of course."

Rosemary digested his comments. They implied he wasn't going to kill her until morning, or later. She construed that as good news until it occurred to her why. She shuddered at the thought of his hands on her body and vowed then and there she would die before she let him take liberties.

"I've always been right fond of yellow hair," Chaco said. "The last blonde I had was a woman on a wagon train that came through about a month and a half ago. She strayed off to gather firewood, and the Mortons and me jumped her and took her to our hiding place. Had us a fine time, we did, before she—"

"Enough!" The vehemence in Rosemary's tone surprised even her. "Spare us your lechery. There's a child present."

"What do I care?" Chaco said, snorting, and looked at Eddy. "How old are you, kid?"

"Nine. But I'll be ten next month."

"Hell, by the time I was ten I'd killed my first man and done things with women that would curl your toes. I remember this one gal, a 'breed like me, she'd do whatever anyone wanted for a dol—"

Reining sharply around, Rosemary coiled to spring. "I won't warn you again." She refused to have her son tainted by their captor's depraved wickedness.

Chaco trained his pistol on her torso. "You're one of those holier-than-thou types, ain't you? Well, it won't make a difference. You'll taste just as sweet. Now, turn that damn cayuse around and keep going."

"Please, Ma," Eddy coaxed when she hesitated. "Don't make him mad."

Rosemary had never despised anyone as much as she despised the weasel holding the gun on her. With every fiber of her being she yearned to tear into him and rip his smug smile from his arrogant face. But she obeyed.

"Smart move," Chaco rasped.

That was all he said for the next half an hour. Other sounds filled the night: the howl of wolves, the bugling of elk, and the occasional grunts of a bear.

From time to time Rosemary surreptitiously glanced at Chaco, praying his guard would lapse so she could attempt to disarm him or distract him long enough for her youngest to flee. But he was as vigilant as a hawk.

"Hold up," Chaco abruptly demanded. He kneed his mount up next to hers and stared intently across the Platte. "This is it. We're going to cross. You and the boy will go ahead of me."

The muzzle of his pistol, pointed at her chest, convinced Rosemary not to argue. The pinto was tentative about entering the flowing water until she flicked her reins a few times and applied her heels. Except for isolated pools, the Platte was as shallow as a river could be and still lay claim to the name. She had a hunch the halfbreed wouldn't pick a deep spot to cross, and she was right. The level rose as high as the pinto's hocks but no farther.

A horseshoe-shaped hill bordered the opposite edge of

the river. The arms of the horseshoe sloped down to the Platte, and between them, flanked by the river on one side and the curved end of the horseshoe on the other, lay a four-acre hideaway effectively screened from the outside world. Sprinkled with trees and brush, it was an ideal hiding place.

"No one can find us here," Chaco bragged, reining toward the horseshoe's west arm. "The boys and me have been using it for months. We only come and go by the river, so we never leave tracks." He cackled at his cleverness. "Smack in the middle of Sioux country, and they have no idea we're here. And it's close enough to the Oregon Trail that we can keep a watch on all the wagon trains that pass by."

Erosion had worn away part of the west arm of the horseshoe, leaving an oval nook approximately ten yards in diameter. Dark as it was, Rosemary distinguished a number of packs, saddlebags, and spare saddles strewn haphazardly about. Occupying the center was the charred remains of a campfire. To its left was a pile of firewood.

"Home, sweet home," Chaco said, and slid to the ground. "Light and sit a spell," he directed, both pistols in his hands now.

Rosemary's leg muscles protested. She was sore and stiff and extremely tired. Her body craved sleep, but her mind had to stay sharp and focused. She went to help Eddy, but he hopped down unaided and came into her outstretched arms.

"How touching," Chaco said in disgust. "When you're done, get the fire going. And just so you won't get your hopes up, it can't be seen from the other side of the river. Or anywhere else, for that matter."

"How am I supposed to start it?" Rosemary said. "Rub two sticks together?"

Chaco wagged a pistol at one of the saddlebags. "There should be a fire steel and flint in there. They belong to Garvey, but I reckon he's past caring if we use them."

One hand pressed to the aching small of her back, Rosemary walked over and knelt. The saddlebag was unfastened. She opened the flap and shoved her fingers into the pocket. They made contact with the fire steel and she slid it out. The flint was harder to find. It was in among fifteen or twenty other articles the saddlebag contained. Her questing fingers brushed something else, an object she instantly recognized for what it was. A quick glance at Chaco showed he was gazing toward the Platte. Quickly, she removed a ten-inch hunting knife in a sheath and shoved it under another saddlebag. None too soon.

"Hurry it up," Chaco groused. "I want some coffee, and I'd like it this year."

Rosemary found the flint. She and Eddy cleared away the charred firewood and added new wood from the pile. A handful of dry grass sufficed for tinder. Hunkering, Rosemary struck the steel and flint together. After a bit, a large spark lodged in the ball of grass, and by lightly puffing on it, she fanned the spark into a tiny flame that rapidly grew in size. Soon the dead wood caught and the fire blazed to life.

"Not bad, lady," Chaco said. He had gone to a pack and was returning with a battered coffeepot. "Here, kid." He threw the pot at Eddy, and although Eddy got his hands up in time, he cried out in pain and dropped the coffeepot at his feet. Chaco cackled, then suddenly fell quiet and motioned for them to do the same.

A second later, Rosemary heard the sounds he had: splashing from the river. Something—or someone—was crossing to their side.

Chaco grabbed Eddy and pushed him toward the fire. "The two of you are to sit there in plain sight and not make a peep." He melted into the darkness, saying, "Remember. I can drop you both anytime I want."

Rosemary draped a protective arm across her youngest's shoulders. "Have faith, Edward," she whispered. "We'll get out of this fix yet. I promise."

"He hurt me, Ma." Eddy held up his left hand. Two of his knuckles were scraped raw and bleeding, and the little finger was swelling.

Right then and there Rosemary Spencer decided that come what may, Ten Commandments or no Ten Commandments, she was going to kill Chaco or die trying. She gave a peck on the cheek and whispered in his ear, "Leave him to me. He's won't ever hurt you again."

Hoof falls thudded dully, and out of the night came a low whinny. A horse and rider took shape, the saddleless mount lathered with sweat, its flanks heaving, an animal on the verge of collapse. The rider wasn't in much better shape. He was bent over, a hand to his side, breathing heavily, with great beads of sweat dotting his bearded face. Reining up, he slowly dismounted. Not until he straightened did he see them, and hatred leapt into his dark eyes. "You!"

Chaco bounded from hiding. "Gault! You made it!" Grinning, he clapped the giant on the arm. "I knew you'd feed that mountain man to the worms."

Wincing, Gault Morton removed his hand from his side. His buckskin shirt was stained with blood. "Don't get ahead of yourself, 'breed. I did no such thing." He limped toward the fire, favoring his left leg. "I was lucky to get out of there with my hide intact. That fella is as hard to shake as my own shadow."

"Nate King is still alive?" Chaco blanched. Nervously licking his thin lips, he scanned the black veil at the mouth of the horseshoe. "What if he followed you here?"

"Relax. He's wounded, same as me. And he didn't know where we stashed the Sioux ponies." Gault sank down with a sigh and pried at his shirt, raising it high enough to examine his wound. A ball had scoured his side, digging a half-inch-deep furrow across his ribs but sparing his vitals. He grunted, then growled, "It's not as bad as I thought. I reckon I'll live after all. But I'm plumb tuckered out."

"I want to know everything that happened."

"There's not much to tell," Gault said wearily. "Garvey and me climbed up on the bluff to cover you, like you wanted. But when we got here, we were considerable surprised to find King and this gal already there, with her runts. We got the drop on them, but they jumped us when I shot the oldest kid. King knifed my brother. I lost my rifle and one of my pistols, so I lit out, but he came after me." He gingerly lowered his shirt. "I got away, and here I am."

"You said King is wounded? Are you sure? Where did you see him last?"

"Relax, I tell you," Gault said irritably. "He chased me through the hills for nigh on an hour. I tried every trick I could think of to shake him, but he dogs a trail like a bloodhound." Gault grimaced. "We took potshots at one another every now and then. One of his clipped me. One of mine caught him as he was skulking over a hill. I saw him fall with my own eyes. He got up again, but he was moving mighty slow."

"Then what?"

"Like I told you. I snuck around to the Sioux horses and came straight here." Gault raised a huge hand when Chaco went to speak. "And yes, I checked my back trail a hundred times. I'd stake my life he wasn't following me."

"That's exactly what's at stake," Chaco said harshly. "Yours and mine, both."

"Even if he's after us, he can't track at night. He'll have to wait until daylight," Gault said, and smirked. "By then we'll be ready for him."

"I won't rest easy until I've touched his dead carcass," Chaco declared. "Mountain men ain't like us. They're more animal than human. And I've heard stories about this King. They say the Utes tried to drive him off for years and gave up. Kicking Bull told me he's the only white man even the Blackfeet won't tangle with."

"He puts his britches on one leg at a time, same as us," Gault said. "Don't make him out to be more than he is."

"Maybe you're right," Chaco said. "We have nothing to worry about until sunrise." Walking over, he kicked Eddy's foot. "Up off your rump, brat, and go fill our coffeepot with water."

"From the river?"

"Unless you can get it from thin air." Chaco seized Eddy by the arm and shoved him with such force, Eddy stumbled and almost fell. "Off you go. And don't dawdle."

Like a tigress springing to the defense of a cub, Rosemary leaped to her feet and sprang. She wasn't fast enough. Chaco whipped around, a pistol squared on her chest, nipping her rush in the bud.

"Sit back down, woman. The kid can do it himself."

Simmering with pent-up fury, Rosemary responded, "He doesn't like being in the dark alone."

"A kid his age? Hell, it ain't that far. And there aren't any grizzlies or cats around. The horses would act up if there were." Chaco gestured at Eddy. "What you waiting for? If I have to tell you again, I'll tan your hide."

Eddy looked forlornly at Rosemary. She smiled and nodded, and he squared his small shoulders and marched off. She listened to the tramp of his feet until the sounds faded. Maternal instinct caused her to take several impulsive steps, but she halted when Chaco barred her way.

"Where the hell do you think you're traipsing off to?"

"He's my son."

"So you coddle him, is that it? Treat him like a baby, even though he's old enough to get by on his own." Chaco moved around the fire so his back was to the hill, and squatted. "I've met your type before, lady. You should have stayed in the States. The frontier ain't for the likes of you."

"What do you know about being a parent?" Rosemary rebutted. "Have you ever had children of your own?" He started to reply, but she didn't let him. "It's obvious you haven't. Because if you had, you'd know that every child is a piece of your heart given life and substance. When they hurt, you hurt. When they cry, you cry. You will do *anything* to safeguard them and ensure they live to have children of their own."

"Well, now," Chaco said derisively, "that was a nice little speech. And to answer your question, no, I've never been a parent. I hope to hell I never am. You see"—his mouth split in a sadistic grin—"I like killing kids, not raising them."

Rosemary's soul recoiled as if brushed by the presence of Satan himself. "You're a monster. A despicable, inhuman monster."

Chaco's laugh was brittle as ice. "I'm every bit as human as you. Only, I don't pretend to be something I'm not. You and your high-and-mighty airs. Always looking down your nose at people like me. I'll show you. Wait until your kid gets back."

Locking her jaw in order not to rile him more, Rosemary folded her arms. She was only a few yards from the knife under the saddlebag. Somehow she must arm herself with it without being noticed.

Tense minutes went by. Rosemary waited expectantly for her youngest to reappear. Chaco glared. Gault was reexamining his wound. Then, from so close by all three of them jumped, came a shrill youthful scream of terror.

"Ma! Ma! Help! It's got me!"

"Eddy!" Rosemary cried, and dashed forward. Before she could take five strides a hand fell on her shoulder, a foot hooked her ankle, and she was flung onto her stomach.

"Where the hell do you think you're going?" Chaco

snarled, and moved past her, his flintlocks leveled.

Gault had risen and was fingering his remaining pistol. "What do you reckon got him? A painter, maybe?"

"How the hell would I know?" Chaco said, and hollered, "Kid, where are you?"

The ensuing silence curdled Rosemary's veins like arsenic in her bloodstream. Her body grew fiery hot, then as chill as the north wind. Her insides churned. Turbulent pounding in her head threatened to smother her consciousness. *She had lost another one! Her husband! Her oldest! And now her precious youngest!* She was all alone. Her future had been dashed to ruin and she had nothing to live for, no reason to go on. *Except revenge.* She glanced at the 'breed and the giant. Neither was paying attention to her. Girding herself, she rose onto her hands and knees and crawled toward the saddlebag. She would get the knife. She would sneak up behind them, bury it in Chaco, and, God willing, live long enough to plunge it into Gault.

Rosemary covered half the distance and glanced back to see if they had noticed. They were still peering into the dark. Another couple of yards and she would have the knife. She faced around and stopped dead. A pair of moccasins had materialized between her and the saddlebags. She was dumbfounded, and her eyes roved upward over the sturdy legs the moccasins were attached to, to a brawny chest and broad shoulders and the handsome head that crowned them. "Nate!" she breathed, in awe and joy.

The mountain man was a terrible sight to behold. His features were set in an iron cast of sheer savagery, and truth to tell, he did appear more beast than man. In his right hand was a pistol, in his left hand his Bowie. "Drop your guns!" he roared in a voice that resounded like steel on burnished bronze.

Chaco started to whirl, thought better of it, and threw his flintlocks to one side. "I should have known!" he said bitterly. "You had the brat yell to distract us!"

Gault turned much more slowly, his hand still on the butt of his flintlock. He didn't act the least bit surprised. "So" was all he said.

Nate King took several steps to the right, placing Rosemary out of the line of fire. "So," he answered, and then, to her disbelief and dismay, he shoved his flintlock under his belt. "Whenever you're ready."

Gault did a strange thing. He smiled, as if in gratitude, and bobbed his chin in a token of respect. "Chaco, if you interfere, I'll kill you my own self." So saying, he streaked his hand to his pistol. His arm a blur, he swept it clear, but it wasn't quite high enough when Nate King's pistol spat smoke and lead and the rear of Gault's cranium showered outward in a spray of gore and brains.

Chaco was in motion before Gault's body crashed to the ground. He leaped toward his pistols, but Nate King blocked his way. Their eyes met. Chaco hissed, and out flashed his long-bladed hunting knife. "I'll do you myself with my blade, then!"

Rosemary opened her mouth to shout for King to watch out, but he had seen the thrust and parried it with his Bowie. King tossed his pistol aside and the two men closed, slashing, cutting, dodging, and ducking almost too fast for her to follow.

Chaco's blade was everywhere, weaving a gleaming tapestry of imminent death. He was confident, quick, and deadly. But soon a change came over him. Rosemary saw his confidence fade, saw bewilderment mushroom into outright fear. And then she saw the most beautiful sight of all: Chaco, fighting for his life. Chaco, pressed inexorably backward by Nate King's glittering Bowie. Chaco, trying a last desperate gambit. Pivoting, he arced his blade up and in. But the Bowie was faster. It cleaved to the hilt into his chest.

Nate King stood over his prone adversary, blood trickling from half a dozen cuts and nicks, and slowly pulled his big knife out.

"You did it!" Rosemary flew to him, wrapped her arms tight.

"Save your hugs," the mountain man said gently. "You'll need them for those two." He shifted, and nodded.

Eddy was approaching, and he wasn't alone. He was supporting Sam, whose shoulder was stained dark but who was as alive as alive could be, and both were grinning from ear to ear.

"Mr. King found me," Sam said. "We came as soon as we could."

"He asked me to scream like that, Ma," Eddy piped up. "I hope you're not mad."

They met in a tangle of arms and tears. Rosemary held them close and gave rein to great choking sobs that took forever to subside. When she finally straightened and turned, Nate had coffee on to brew. She made no attempt to hide the feelings her eyes betrayed.

The mountain man deliberately looked off into the distance. "Come morning I'll take you to Fort Laramie. You'll be able to get all the help you need there."

"Is that all?"

"Then it's on to the Rockies for me. I have a wife waiting, remember? I've been away from her too long as it is."

Rosemary Spencer put on a brave smile. "I'm happy for you, Mr. King. I truly am." She sucked in a deep breath and switched her smile to her sons. "Samuel, let's bandage you up and have some supper. We all need a good night's sleep. Tomorrow is the start of a whole new life."

WILDERNESS

#25
FRONTIER MAYHEM

<----------------------------------->

David Thompson

The unforgiving wilderness of the Rocky Mountains forces a boy to grow up fast, so Nate King taught his son, Zach, how to survive the constant hazards and hardships—and he taught him well. With an Indian war party on the prowl and a marauding grizzly on the loose, young Zach is about to face the test of his life, with no room for failure. But there is one danger Nate hasn't prepared Zach for—a beautiful girl with blue eyes.

___4433-1 $3.99 US/$4.99 CAN

WILDERNESS

BLOOD FEUD

David Thompson

The brutal wilderness of the Rocky Mountains can be deadly to those unaccustomed to its dangers. So when a clan of travelers from the hill country back East arrive at Nate King's part of the mountain, Nate is more than willing to lend a hand and show them some hospitality. He has no way of knowing that this clan is used to fighting—and killing— for what they want. And they want Nate's land for their own!

___4477-3 $3.99 US/$4.99 CAN